Welling
City Blues

Adam Hankinson

SRL Publishing Ltd

SRL Publishing Ltd
London
www.srlpublishing.co.uk

First published worldwide by SRL Publishing in 2022

ISBN: 978-183827989-9

1 3 5 7 9 10 8 6 4 2

A CIP catalogue record for this book is available from the
British Library

SRL Publishing is a Climate Positive publisher, removing more
carbon emissions than it emits.

Dedicated to Ty Mcnaughton
Fallen brother
Rising angel

Chapter 1

*For some reason it dawned on me I hadn't seen the blue sky in
what felt like a decade. No one had, not that anybody had the time
to ponder the land and listen to the sound of its voice. New age
spiritualists claimed they heard the voice of Gaia singing her earthly
melodies of wind whistling through trees and water trickling down
rocks, but I heard different, saw different. For I have watched my
people slowly decay in their slumber, with glass pipes pressed to
cracking lips, fading into the smoke soon to vanish like their very
existence. For I have rested my eyes on the dark of all dark which
is our death.*

"Corey Gnosis"

Homeless Harry use to say music was the window to the
soul. He always said we were the conductors to the
symphony we call life, and for most it being a sombre
melody with no uplifting chorus, just a drawn-out verse
hoping to reach a climatic end. Homeless Harry would sit
at the foot of two ram-shackled buildings in the outskirts

of town, a cigarette hanging out the side of his mouth, his eyes hidden behind his reflective lens, and he'd press his weary sax to his lips and blow the saddest, truest notes you'd hear in no other place than Wellington city. He played songs that would melt your heart, bring tears to your eyes, and force you to ponder your existence.

In-between late night jamming sessions, Harry would stand at the mouth of some sleazy alley while people threw coins at his feet. He would tell me how music flows through, and out of us, inevitably making its way back, for good or for worse. Through Harry's lens we were all products of our environment, displaced onto tiny patches of land we would call our homes. He saw life as a series of suffering, our way of being amidst the suffering was the result of our musical composition.

He quickly realized the pull the Yin had over the Yang, and how the life he envisioned was completely out of reach. Drugs and alcohol became the only viable escape to his desired paradise. But instead, he was led down a darkened path where the city folk tossed their burdens off their backs and piled them on top of him and his saxophone. Homeless Harry absorbed the cruel vibrations of the city, articulating them through his blues that, eventually, he would call: *Wellington city blues.*

Like Harry, I ended up on the streets when I was a teenager. As my father put it, "my presence was murderous." My mother died giving birth to me, my old man never forgave me. He said she was the only person who brought joy into his life. As a result of the loss, he turned to the bottle in hope of finding a cure, but all alcohol ever did was make his fists busy. At the age of five, I was taken out of his volatile hands and passed onto a foster family who held strong Christian convictions. They enrolled me into Saint Aberdeen's boy's college, which was like a never-ending Sunday church ceremony.

For my own entertainment I ran amuck with a bright eyed, ginger haired boy called Tony, who also had trouble fitting in. One thing I could never forget about Tony was his smile. When he smiled, it looked like a thousand smart-ass kids gelled into one incredibly cheeky expression. We both came from foster homes, so it goes without saying we went together like bread and butter.

Tony was a lot taller than the other boys, but he didn't have the muscular upper body to vouch for his figure, the kids gave him hell, called him *stretch* and all kinds of nasty names. But he couldn't care less, that was what drew me to him in the first place. He always told me he felt like a stranger to the world, yet still, he gave everyone a dose of his uniqueness, despite what the clones said or did to him.

Tony not only introduced me to friendship, but to a world I never knew existed. I had my first beer with Tony, I smoked my first joint with Tony, and I shot dope for the first time, yes, with Tony. Ever since then, my life was never the same. I no longer identified with the person I was before. Drugs spin you around in circles with a blindfold wrapped around your eyes, as much as you try, you'll never find your way back to the person you were before the very first hit.

3

The sudden shift in attitude led to Tony and my expulsion from Saint Aberdeen's. It turned out my foster mum was close with the principle, out of fear for her reputation as a good Christian woman she disowned me. I was booted to social services and sent to an alternative school. Things didn't exactly go to plan, not that I had one to begin with. When you throw a *troubled kid* into a room full of other *troubled kids*, you can't help but create someone competent in the field of defiance.

Eventually the court sentenced me to Residence (a nice name for juvenile prison), there, I did the only thing I could at the time, escape, in search for my freedom. But as I quickly learned, freedom isn't at all what it's cracked up to be. I was left alone on the street with no money and nothing to eat, the only company I had were the memories of my past, soulless junkies, and other strange creatures who quietly boiled away at everybody's feet.

After drifting around my friend's couches (more than once) until they grew sick of me, I fled to the city, finding my solace beside restaurant bins, filling the long, cold days with people watching. To begin with, I held onto my pride and hid away at the park for most of the day until the skies bruised, then I felt comfortable enough to crawl back into the city to hide in the shadows for a nap. Sooner or later, I became accustomed to my newfound world, freely sliding down the social ladder, but this time I didn't feel alienated. I came to terms with my present condition, knowing things would change the way the days of the week do. I wasn't one hundred percent sure of this, but it was all I had to keep me going.

4

Homeless Harry took me under his wing from the very start, he showed me the ropes, the *do's*, the *dont's*, and how to survive. Like any good master he left me to fend for myself so I could survive long after he faded away. But he always manifested when I needed him the most, bringing with him a bread roll and a shoulder to lean on.

I'd seen many dull days that'd pass you by without any second thoughts, but on this one day in particular my life would begin to change in unimaginable ways…

On this day, I zipped my grey overcoat all the way up to my throat, wishing the zip would carry on all the way over my head so I would disappear. The zip put alarming pressure on my throat, yet I found comfort from the lack of oxygen flowing into my dirty lungs. *Maybe if this thing went a little tighter, I could kill myself*, I thought. That way I wouldn't have to deal with my moaning stomach, the pungent stench emanating off my overcoat, and the endless coastal gusts. My jacket hardly did its job of providing warmth anyhow. It felt like a withered layer of skin protecting my soon to decay body.

I rested my head on the filthy bricks outside the Bristol bar on Cuba Street, watching the commuters strut along the pavement with their phones pressed to their ears, catching the glimmer of certainty present in their eyes. Most were dressed in their business attire, staring confidently into the future, seeing no more than the path to success that would not bend, crack, or wind. It just led straight, straight up steel framed buildings and ceased at the final floor. After all those years gone by, they're left thinking, *cool, now what?*

Blurry eyed people passed me by pressing headphones into their ears in hope of escaping to another galaxy. I didn't blame them. If I had a phone—or some money—I'd be doing my best to distract myself from this bleak existence as well. But there I was, another soulless bum, meditating on the street's day and night, on the side-line of life, watching the hordes of pretenders carry out their affairs. I wished I had a cigarette. No matter what adversity life threw at you, everything would be okay if you had a cigarette.

From afar, I watched some corporate junkie bark into his phone while stubbing out the butt of his smoke with his Italian leather shoes. I watched on like a starving hyena, waiting for my moment to strike. There were still a good couple of drags left, and even better, it still had a few embers to work with. I staggered over and plucked the butt off the ground as if someone had dropped a diamond. Taking rapid puffs, I held the smoke in my lungs, releasing a euphoric sigh as a small cloud of smoke dispersed into the chilling air.

People with clean silky hair and short fingernails pretended they didn't notice my stealthy scavenge. But their hollow eyes told me they well and truly witnessed my step toward social degradation. I didn't care what they thought. If they didn't judge me today, they'd judge me tomorrow.

As the days grew shorter and the nights seemed eternal, eventually I lost my compass on time. But I gained a rough idea of what day it was by listening to the vibration of the city. For example, Monday had a feel of hopelessness, Tuesday was caged, Wednesday brought upon the ease of a downhill hike, most people got paid Thursday so everyone was buying lunch and drinking at bars after work—sometimes they'd drop coins at my feet. Friday was the day where everyone discovered their sense of humour and decided to be nice to each other. Saturday would be the day of celebrations, big spending, until it collapsed into an alcohol induced coma. People let the monkey out the cage, inebriated chaos would unfold until the holy sun of Sunday brought them back to life.

I stopped outside an electronics shop with wide screen TVs displayed in the windows broadcasting news updates. No doubt, the reporters were discussing New Zealand's skyrocketing youth suicide rate.

A blonde middle-aged woman dressed in a black pencil skirt with a matching blouse stopped and stared at the television. I figured she had kids and was concerned for their wellbeing, or otherwise knew someone who had committed suicide. In New Zealand, just about everyone knows someone, who knows someone, who has committed suicide. It was quite surreal to hear people reporting about it, a topic richly suppressed and hidden away like razor blade scars on your arms. But, unlike razor blade scars, the crisis wouldn't be resolved until the heart of the matter was healed.

Something about hearing the news update repelled me from the city. I felt like the city itself was a breeding zone for self-destruction. It was then I decided at first light the following morning, I'd leave the city behind and begin the long trek inland to a place where a different kind of insanity rocked the town-folk into a hazy unrest. I needed a change in scenery, I needed to find a place where life moved slower, a place where I belonged. Little did I know I was on the brink of embarking on a journey that would change my life forever.

Chapter 2

At sunrise I strapped my backpack over one shoulder and followed the highways north. I could have hitch-hiked, but there was nothing on my plate to be hungry about. Walking felt delightful, all the different angles and outlooks of the city from afar made it actually look beautiful. Nonetheless, I kept on hiking until the buildings got smaller and the traffic thinned out. For the first time I felt purpose, even if that purpose was simply trekking into the Hutt Valley suburbs, it was something for me to hang on to.

It took me half the day to walk to Lower Hutt, which was like a slice of Wellington overrun with hoodlums, careless punks who wouldn't hesitate to shatter your jaw. It was a different kind of hustle bustle. Instead of everyone flailing in the city rip, the people appeared to be floating in stagnant waters. If the streets had a voice, it would be screaming, *What's mine is mine! What's yours is my desires!*

I bought a loaf of bread from the supermarket for a dollar, slapping a handful of loose change on the counter in which the clerk had to count. Once my stomach was clogged with bread, I marched out of town following the Hutt River upstream. Somewhere in-between Pomare and Stokes Valley, I peeled off my foul clothes and took a quick bath in the icy water as the sun set behind the hills. It was a view I'd never forget. The weakened sun setting into the valley like a giant ball of light sinking into a bowl of earth. Shivering, I threw on my clothes, hugging my knees before falling into dreams of snow-capped mountains.

The following morning, I arose with the sun, feeling sluggish and beat, like a bunch of hood-rats spent the evening taking turns stomping on my ribs. There was nothing on my mind asides from a tall glass of water, but the river was too murky to drink—let alone wash in. As I edged closer to the mouth of the valley, Amber popped into my mind. I met Amber through Tony a year before I was kicked out of Aberdeen College. She lived in a rickety flat on stilts in the Valley Heights—a strenuous climb on an almost vertical road at the entrance of the valley.

In the past we spent just about every waking minute together. Quite often, I'd stay at her place for weeks on end as my attendance at school slowly declined. Her mother worked in Australia doing fly-in-fly-out work on a mining site, so Amber had the place to herself, her mum paid the bills and sent her money every week. We blew her weekly allowance on weed and alcohol (done up in make-up, Amber looked at least twenty-one).

Amber had issues and not the average kind. I knew this because she spilled her heart out to me when she was punch drunk one night. I remember her telling me when she was a girl her stepdad used to read her favourite story before bed. It was about a pony who had lost its way home. The pony followed a never-ending dirt trail where other animals helped her along the way—some animals even deceived the pony. At the end of the story, her stepdad would give her a kiss and tuck her in nice and snug. I didn't know what happened next, but I could have guessed. Before she could finish the story, Amber broke down until she eventually cried herself to sleep. I tried to comfort her, but my touch only seemed to make matters worse.

Not too long after, alcohol wasn't strong enough, so she moved onto harder drugs which were easily accessible in our hometown. Within weeks, Amber faded away and I, too, became a ghost to her.

As I staggered up the gruelling hill, I wondered if I was making the wrong decision. Too much time had passed between us, I thought. Maybe we weren't the same kids we used to be. I didn't really have much of a choice, though. My body was operating on instinct, and before I knew it, I wound up outside her flat. Food wouldn't be on the table, but she had a tap that poured unlimited mouthfuls of sweet tasting water.

The door was left wide open as if she were expecting someone to arrive. At this stage, my shoes felt like they were made of cement, and I couldn't wait to flick them

11

off and put my feet up. A decrepit pit-bull, I knew as Rotness, stuck his nose out the door. I could see he wanted to unleash his most vicious bark at me, but the poor fella didn't even have the strength to do so. As I introduced myself, the way I would to a stranger, he settled down and dropped with a thud on the chewed-up carpet.

In his prime he would have been a gorgeous dog with a luminous black coat with muscular arms and legs. But now I could see the outline of his ribcage. It saddened me to see a dog so young look like he had reached the end of the line. I took a knee and ran a hand down his spine. It felt like I was stroking nothing more than bones, he didn't appear to be getting any satisfaction from it, so I left him in peace.

'Amber!' I called out, tuning into the vibrations of the house. I felt nothing. There was no presence, no atmosphere, just the hollowness of empty time that had passed by. 'Where is she, boy?' I asked Rotness.

His ears pricked up sluggishly, then he fell back into his slumber.

To my surprise the place looked immaculate. The black granite benchtops speckled with white dots sparkled like the stars I use to gaze at when I was a kid. The pantries were efficiently organized, colour coordinated and all, the carpet was routinely vacuumed despite poor old Rotness trying to chew it up for dinner. In fact, the lounge was so clean, I felt obliged to take off my shoes and leave them on the porch.

I poured myself a glass of water and gulped it down,

fixing myself another. Once I quenched my thirst, I raided the pantry. The shelves were left bare as expected, but I did manage to find a small bag of dog food. I filled up Rotness's bowl and he stumbled over. He drove his nose into the bowl, fiendishly licking it clean.

'Feel any better, boy?' I asked.

He wagged his tail, hitting the bowl with his nose, telling me he wanted more.

'Sorry boy, that's all there is.'

I got lost in the fantasy of taking him with me. I'd share my can of baked beans with him, wrap him up in my coat on the riverside as we watched the motionless clouds swallow the land. But how irresponsible would that be? Here, he has shelter and a bowl filled with… I stared at his food bowl that was clean, too clean… Who am I kidding, neither of us can take care of ourselves. Rotness would be better off without us.

With a newfound spring in his step, Rotness approached the hallway, stopping midway to catch my eye, as if saying, *follow me*. I followed him down the hall and he pawed at the door. I patted him on the head and knocked two times.

'Amber! Are you in there?… I'm coming in!'

I pushed open the door, half expecting to see Amber decomposing on the bedroom floor. She was alive and breathing but looked like death had been paying her weekly visits. Her body shook in fright midway through sucking on a glass pipe. Choking on the body rot she managed to blurt out my name. 'Corey? Is that you?'

I forced a smile.

She looked like she hadn't slept in years. Her skin was ghostly, like she was an apparition trapped in the physical realm, her cheek bones protruded off her face making her look like a skeleton. She fetched a hairbrush and leaped to the nearest mirror, running the brush through her long black hair. I stood in the doorway with my arms crossed, wondering how many days she had gone on like this.

'The place looks nice,' I said finally. 'Maybe next you could clean yourself up.'

I didn't come here to give her a lecture, who am I to judge? But it came from a place within my heart.

Her face creased. I could see all the burdens she carried brewing up inside of her. She frowned, about to spew her demons upon me. But before she erupted, I pulled her in for a hug. Her skinny little body relaxed in my arms, and she buried her face into my chest. Her eyes turned innocent. I could see her inner child crying out from behind those brown eyes. Her eyes foretold the years of hardship she had endured. Amber was like a tree trying to grow within a cyclone, hanging onto dear life by her frail roots, yet praying for one mighty gust to rip her roots away from the earth.

She pulled away from me. The way she did to everyone who got too close.

'Are you forgetting something,' I said, gesturing to Rotness.

Revitalized, Rotness pounced up at me, trying to give me a slobbery kiss.

'I've forgotten everyone,' Amber said, withdrawing

14

her tears. 'I don't know who I am anymore, Corey.'

'What happened to your carpentry job?' I asked. 'Last time I saw you, you were rearing to fix the world.'

There was a lagging silence. I figured she reflected on her former self, the self she placed into a pipe and burnt to ashes.

'I quit. I was going to let them down anyway, so I thought I'd put them out of their misery.'

'Amber…' I said, treading tenderly over my next words. 'You're better than that, and you know it. Don't throw in the towel so soon. Even if you were defeated, learn from your mistakes, come back stronger—'

'Like you can talk, Corey!'

Her searing words set light to my optimism. I don't know if I believed in what I said—she sure as hell didn't.

Furiously packing the pipe with more crystals, she snarled, 'Never thought I'd be receiving advice from a bum. How is Wellington city treating you, anyway? Get tired of always being in the way of everyone, huh? So you decided to come back home to see there's pieces of shit out there worse off than you?'

I shook my head, stunned by her outburst. I didn't come here to be saintly. In all honesty, I wanted a glass of water, maybe some food to eat. While I was here, I thought I may as well check to see if she had built herself a coffin.

'No, not at all!' I protested. 'My situation is living proof you can overcome anything. I'm a nobody, a nobody who still lives to see another day.'

'What's so brilliant about being able to *see another day*?'

She exhaled a thin cloud of smoke. Shooting herself in the face yet again, she sparked another crooked crystal. 'Is *that* a valid reason to live? To see another day? The only person you are fooling is yourself, and all the fuck-wits who are stupid enough to smoke your words.' She fumbled with her lighter. The flame had given up on her. She clicked, shook, and sparked it several times before throwing it at the wall. 'We're digging our own graves here, Corey. Each and every day that passes, my grave looks more inviting, that there is paradise, one great big eternal sleep. No feelings, no people stirring your shit, no commitments, no letting people down, and above all, no more days, weeks, years…'

I wanted to pull her back into my chest so our broken hearts could form a whole. But I feared her heart had slipped out of place long ago. Too many people had treaded over it, to the point of it being beyond repair.

Her words rang truth to how a lot of people felt down here. I felt the same at times. We all had our own ways of dealing with the unfavourable circumstances of life. I hung onto falling stars and descended the heavens, heading straight for oblivion until I let go and leaped to another star before it combusted. As for Amber, death seemed to be her only option, her only way forward, tearing out the final page of her life and laying it to waste.

I then saw a flicker of remorse in her far away eyes. 'You can stay… but no more of this preacher shit, okay?'

'Thanks,' I said, my heart drooping down my sleeve.

'You want a shower?' she asked. 'You smell like shit.'

Without a word, I took off my clothes and left them

16

in a pile on the floor. I had no shame. Homelessness in the city had taught me that. The water was just as cold as the Hutt River. Amber stopped paying her electricity bill a couple of months ago so she had more money for meth. Turned out her mother cut her off when she returned home last Christmas. Living on welfare checks meant slim living, even if you lived somewhat of a functional life.

After two minutes in the shower, I couldn't take any more of it. I managed to lather up my body with soap and rinse off, but didn't quite make it to washing my shaggy blond hair. As I dried myself, I realized the bathtub tap was running. I couldn't think of anything worse at this point of time. Amber came in holding a pot of hot water she'd boiled on the stove top. She poured it in the tub and went back to the kitchen to boil more.

'Get in!' her voice echoed from the kitchen.

'I'm not getting in that thing, you're dreaming!'

She charged back into the bathroom with another pot of hot water. 'I thought you wouldn't last too long in the shower. So I thought a hot bath would sort you out. How long has it been?'

I didn't answer her question. Mainly because it had been so long, I'd forgotten. After she poured two more pots of hot water in the bath I eased into the tub. The moment the water touched my skin I felt a thousand hands massage every muscle in my body.

'Good, aye?' said Amber, grinning.

Her smile, I thought. I forgot what she looked like when she was genuinely happy. Through her smile I saw what she would have looked like as a little girl, that is, before scaly hands spilled their lustful desires over her, and caused a stain they didn't care enough about to wash out.

'Here, use as much as you want.' She biffed a bottle of shampoo at me. 'You're not sleeping in my bed until you wash that greasy mop of yours.'

Once the water turned to ice, I hopped out, wrapped a towel around my body and retraced my steps to the bedroom to grab my clothes. But they were gone. I heard the hose running in the backyard, so I made my way to the back patio and stepped out onto the frosty grass. My clothes were pinned up on the line with a few scoops of washing powder thrown over them, while Amber gunned them down with the hose.

'What the hell are you doing? They'll take days to dry in this weather!'

Blasting my overcoat with a little too much enthusiasm she said, 'You're staying a while, aren't ya?' She smiled, her brown eyes glistening.

I nodded. I didn't want to bring her down, obviously she had been without good company for a while. My plans were to continue trekking north into Upper Hutt, for no other reason than being closer to nature—and to be at a safe distance from the city. Nevertheless, I lied and said I would stay.

Dropping the hose, she hurried over to me, her gumboots splashing in the puddles caught within the cobblestone. She wrapped her arms around my shoulders, squishing her cheek into my collarbone. I felt strained of movement and got the feeling my boots would be sitting on the shoe rack for some time. My broadening horizons shrunk in size. Being foot loose was always overshadowed by comfortability, its worst enemy.

I felt guilty for wanting to get on my way and continue my suburban odyssey. But Amber and I had history. We had been through a bit more than sharing a midnight pipe every so often on dole day. For starters, we survived adolescence together—and boy, was that a dangerous ride. Side by side, we built our wall of defence against the world by burning bundles of weed to ward off the evil spirits of reality. Booze, weed, and psychedelics created a private universe for us and our small group of friends. But eventually the drugs stopped working. People shape-shifted into fiendish ghouls, and the clan of no-good punks dressed in black fell to its death.

Isolation's a killer. Paranoia is a bookmark stuck between the pages of an unread book. Once upon a time, we were brave, the ones who dared to see what was on the other side. But how quickly our bravery became ignorance, escapism, and suicidal ideations.

Chapter 3

Amber offered to buy me dinner, she had a little money left over before her next welfare check rolled in, but we both quickly changed our minds when we drove past the liquor store. I patted my stomach and thought there was no way it could get any smaller. It was a choice between looking after my head, or my stomach. Go figure.

I stayed in the car because I was dressed in Amber's pink fluffy dressing gown (my clothes were still drip drying on the line). She waltzed out of the liquor store with a bottle of bourbon in one hand, and a pack of Pall Mall's in the other. The only ingredients necessary for a cold winter's night in the suburbs.

We drank in her car and played the same music we used to listen to back in the *good old days*. But for some reason the songs didn't ring true to me the way they used to. I watched Amber bob her head to the grooves, all starry eyed and caught in the moment. I found myself caught somewhere in-between the person I once was—or at least thought I was—and the desolation I couldn't quite shake off my back. It may have been the bourbon flowing through my blood, but it dawned on me for the past twenty years I had been living a lie, an elaborate façade only I could understand, feel and perceive, alone. Everywhere I turned I felt the eyes of judgment upon me. From eyes in the sky, to the petty judgments below. What good was I doing hanging around with Amber anyway? My mere presence reinforced her old habits— and my old habit's—providing plastic hope and an excuse to withdraw. She'd figure it out soon enough.

Around midnight Amber passed out on the couch beside me—weeks of sleepless nights are bound to catch up on you. I polished off the bottle and sat on the porch beneath the weak glow of a streetlamp and wept. They were selfish tears. Tears over my life sentencing on this beautiful earth, this beautiful prison for souls.

I threw a blanket over Amber, giving her a kiss on the forehead. I watched her sleep for a few moments so I wouldn't forget this snapshot in time, for when I'm alone on the river's edge, I would resurface this memory of a special time, when I had someone by my side who heard my voice, someone who looked me in the eye, and not through me. Tomorrow when Amber awoke, I would be gone. If I decided to stay, she would hate me by the end of the week, anyway. Leaving was a decision I made with our best interests at heart.

The sun was due to rise in a couple of hours. I was still drunk and that was a part of the plan, beat the morning traffic, and enjoy the quietness of dawn. Come to think about it, I was beginning to miss the simplicity of life on the riverside, resting my head on rocks, having conversations with the birds, and the busy rivers determination to flow, and do nothing other than flow with the rhythms of nature.

I fetched the ashtray off the coffee table, along with rolling papers and filter tips. I broke apart the butts and recycled the tobacco. My clothes were still drip drying on the line, I shuddered at the thought of being in wet clothes. I made a coffee and sat on the porch, watching the silent brushes of orange form in the sky.

Before I got changed, I took my clothes into the bathroom and strained them into the bathtub. The water running out of the clothes was a murky brown. I turned on the tap and washed it down the drain, not wanting to investigate the matter any further. With my wet clothes on my back, I felt a couple of kilograms heavier, I just hoped the wind would dry them out as I walked. As a vagrant you were prone to suffering, it was inevitable and would prove to test your endurance, so being left out to dry like a wet sponge meant nothing more than a stone was in my shoe.

Last night I let it slip to Amber about my plans of hiking into Upper Hutt and beyond. She was in such a state she pulled apart her storage closet. She insisted I took with me a large, but lightweight tarp, perfect for a make-shift shelter, as well as some frail looking guy-rope and a tent. I tucked them into the side of my pack, feeling nervous suddenly. As I strapped on my boots, I thought about how we were so deep into winter, rainfall was no longer a question. The equipment I acquired was essential and would prove to be in the coming days.

I sifted through my gear, taking mental note of everything. One plastic rain-poncho (they were handing them out at the soup kitchen in the city), one Bic lighter (collected after a drunk dropped it), four slices of mouldy bread (I'd pick off the mould later), a one-day pass for the train (expired) but the cardboard could be used to start a fire. An empty leather wallet (could use it to keep things dry), and of course the stuff Amber gave me.

I continued to dig into the bottom of my pack. I found a compact sleeping bag; Amber must've slipped it in when I wasn't looking. Maybe she sensed I was going to leave when I told her about my plans. I still don't know, but it was something to think about as I took the first couple of steps down the Valley Heights.

The streetlamps burnt out, and I was left in an airy blue darkness. The odd person strolled past walking their dog, but other than that I had the sidewalk to myself. Half a dozen cars whooshed past, some bashed their horns and gave me the fingers, others watched on curiously. I followed the Eastern Hutt Road until I dipped down a hillside, linking up with the river trail—a smooth path leading all the way to Emerald Hill and beyond.

The clouds were angry and awfully low, resting on the surrounding hilltops. Based on the purple and grey tinges present, it looked like it would rain for days. I wasn't going to allow this notion to diminish my progress, so I made a quick pact with myself to not stop underneath a tree to build a shelter. Not that the trees on the riverside offered much shelter. All I saw for miles were an array of skeleton trees, hanging by their roots on the riverbank, stripped of springs compliments.

The last thing I wanted was to stop in the middle of the rain to eat lunch. So I fished out the loaf of bread and plucked out the mould growing around the crust. But there was more mould than I thought. *Who cares*, I thought, scoffing back the last of the bread. It's all energy some way or another.

By this point the clouds looked like death swarming in the sky. I smoked a cigarette all the way to the filter, hurled on my pack, and slipped into my rain-poncho. I smiled to myself as the strange feeling of purpose warmed up my stomach.

Hell, I could trek all the way around the North Island, no sweat, I thought.

The clouds rumbled and I saw a flash of light, then suddenly, the clouds burst and the skies became a giant shower head, dampening my thoughts of train hopping around the country. How blind I was then. Nothing ever is the way it seems, and life most certainly never flows like this river.

***

I couldn't take it anymore. I felt the cold festering into my bones. I couldn't walk properly, my legs refused to stop shaking. This was supposed to be simple, following a relatively easy path north. How did everything turn upside down? Who would have thought water could cause so much damage?

The river turned an awful brown and flowed faster than I could run. It was rising higher up the bank every hour. My boots were caked in mud, my socks wet, for the trail had become a boggy nightmare. I thought I was prepared for this. If I was back in the city, I would have had an abundance of resources to work with given this situation. But that's in the urban kingdom of man, here it's a wild flooded hellhole.

I didn't have much of a choice other than to head back into town. I was fuming because I was carrying nothing but choice a few moments ago, but where did my will go? Probably down the river and back to the very start of the story.

Back on the highway, I figured I was somewhere in-between Silverstream and Trentham. Realistically, I hadn't covered much ground at all—and by the look of the traffic it was well past lunchtime. I was yet to find a place to sleep and the countdown to sunset had already begun. *It would be a lot easier to think if the rain buggered off*, I thought.

A van tooted at me and pulled to the side of the road. A middle-aged man wearing a high-visibility vest rolled down the passenger window.

'Jump in! The side door's open, just mind the tools!'

I didn't think twice and leaped through the sliding door. Warmth and dryness were completely foreign to me at this point, he had the internal heater system pumping on full. I was in the van for only a couple of seconds, but already formed a puddle of water on the floor, though the guy didn't seem to care.

'Where ye headin'?' he asked, pulling back onto the road.

'Good question,' I admitted.

'There's a train station further up, could drop ya there.'

A train station, that means shelter, I thought. 'Sure, train station it is.' I then remembered my expired day pass. Maybe I could try my luck and tamper with the date, then I could have a crack at venturing further up the line.

'Name's Wayno,' the guy said.

'Corey,' I replied.

'I work on a construction site just past the racecourse. We work in all kinds of weather. But today, we got sent home. So, tell me, Corey, what the fuck are you doing walking along a highway in this weather?'

'Long story,' I said.

Wayno nodded his head as if he understood what I meant. He put a cigarette in-between his lips. 'Want one?'

'Nah, I've got some in my bag, but thanks.'

'Take one,' he insisted, holding the packet over his shoulder, his other hand on the wheel. 'Ya smokes'll be fucked from the rain.'

I took up his offer. Once again, his hand reached over his shoulder. This time he held a can of Smirnoff Ice. 'Have a drink, kid. You look like you need it.'

'Thanks, man,' I said, clawing at the tab.

He dropped me off at Trentham station and swung around to see me off. It was the first time I properly saw his face, which looked like it was made of leather and sandpaper, but his eyes were blue and gentle. 'All the best, mate,' he said.

I thanked him and jumped out the van, landing in a puddle which sprayed up my leg.

'Oi, kid!' he called out.

I spun around in just enough time to catch a flying Smirnoff. He tooted his horn and disappeared into the fog.

I took off my poncho and left it to dry on the seat beside me. The next train was due in fifteen minutes, the service terminated in Upper Hutt. *Fifteen minutes to find a pen*, I thought, scouting out the potential passengers. There were none. I should have known; Trentham was generally a deserted stop—at least throughout the day. Further down the platform, a door clicked open, then I heard a bunch of keys rattling. It was a Kiwi-Rail employee waiting to be picked up by the next train.

'Excuse me!' I shouted, running up to him. Panting, I said, 'Pen… could I use it…'

'Ah, you can have it,' said the rail worker, who took a few steps away from me.

I retreated to the end of the platform, planting myself beside my poncho which was still dripping off water. I grabbed my wallet out of my bag where the all-day pass was stored. Thankfully, it was dry, as well as every other item in the bag. The ticket was for 01/08/2020. But what was todays date? Depending on what day it was, determined whether my plan succeeded or failed.

I called out to the rail worker who was now on the far end of the platform.

'Hey! Excuse me! What's the date?'

'The 10th of August 2020, planet earth!' He shouted.

'Thank you!'

Somehow, I had to add on a zero to the one. But the one was pushed to the side by a zero. *It's useless*, I thought. There's no way to forge it unless the ticket-master was blind. The train was due any second. I folded up my poncho and put it back in its plastic casing.

I decided to hop on the train anyway, I'd just partially cover up the date on the ticket. Ideally, I wanted to end up in Upper Hutt. If I fell short, that would mean I'd have to walk in the rain into town as the sun set, meaning I'd be in the danger zone for getting hypothermia. All I could do was hand my fate over to the God of everything trains and tickets, and pray he showed me mercy.

The train rolled in right on schedule. The carriages were stuffed with passengers, mainly students coming back from uni. I headed for the far carriage to the left, keeping a close eye on the ticket-masters who worked either end of the train. The ticket-master closest to me locked eyes with me as I jumped on.

'Shit,' I said to myself, as I searched for a seat far away from him. I knew that look. I had seen it too many times to count. Policemen and security guards often gave me that look in the city. The look that said, *I'm watching you*.

I squeezed into a seat next to an elderly woman. The old woman smiled warmly, then peered out the window as we whooshed past the suburbs. At least they couldn't throw me off in-between stations the way they used to.

Either way, I was still covering good ground.

The snake eyed ticket-master came at me in slow motion. I could see the determination in his face, the authority in his step, he flicked his ticket-clippers out of his belt like it were a pistol in a holster, and gave it a few audible *clicks*. I drew upon my ticket from my wallet, holding it close to my hip like a weapon, bracing myself for the standoff.

'Ticket please,' he said, staring right through me.

I held my ticket at eye level, ever so slightly covering the date.

He held out his hand, wanting to take a closer look.

My hand froze in mid-air, hoping he would hurry up and say, *thank you, have a good day*.

He pinched the ticket out of my hand, taking his time to inspect it.

I held my breath.

'It was issued to me today,' I broke in. 'The ticket printer must have had some malfunction.'

'Malfunction?' said the ticket-master, raising an eyebrow. 'Let's see what my scanner has to say about that.' He unclipped a handheld decoder from his utility belt and scanned the transaction. 'Nope,' he said gravely. 'There's no malfunction. Just standard human error.'

Curse technology, I thought.

'Ester,' he said into his walkie-talkie. 'Inform security we've got a free-loader, over.'

He stared at me like I just killed a man. 'We will take you as far as Wallaceville station. There, security will take note of your infringement and hand out your fine.'

Flustered, I said, 'Fine?'

'Yes. This is a criminal offense.'

'And how do you expect me to pay it? With the change people drop into my hat?'

'You can discuss the matter further with security at the station.' He mentally slammed a door shut between us and stood by my side until the train reached the next stop. The brakes whined and the train began to slow down. I swung my bag over one shoulder and headed for the door.

'Oh no you don't!' snapped the ticket master. 'You're to stay by my side until we escort you to rail security.' As the train came to a halt, I caught sight of two morbidly obese security guards a few carriages down. The ticket-master gripped the fabric on the top of my pack and steered me toward them.

'This is him! Over here!' he shouted.

It felt like a century had passed before security finally hauled their bodies over to us.

'I'll let you guys take it from here,' said the ticket-master, stepping back aboard the train.

'Okay,' said one of the guards, fishing out a pen and pad from his pocket. He sounded like he had a mouthful of food stored in the side of his mouth when he spoke. 'We just need some personal information. Your full name for starters, followed by your address.'

I weighed up my escape routes. Behind me were the train tracks, and a barb wired fence separating me from the suburbs. There's no way in hell these guards would jump down on the tracks—let alone climb a barb wired fence. But then again, once I cleared the fence, I had to jump over yet another fence into someone's backyard, where anything could be waiting for me on the other side. In front of me was a slim path leading to the station's car park. The easiest way out. But the thing was, I had two whales on either side of me, blocking the most obvious means of escape.

'Oi, I'm not gonna say it again, full name and address?' the guard with rolls around his forehead grumbled.

'Noneaya,' I began, 'Noneaya Business.'

The security guard jotted it down. 'How you spell that? Is it French?'

My moment was now. I curled up into a ball and rolled in between the guards. Both guards went for me at the same time, bashing their bellies together as they swayed like imbalanced spinning tops. Seeing nothing but the openness of the car park, I ran for my life. They chased after me for two meters before stopping to catch their breath as if they just ran a marathon. All they could do was watch me glide along the puddles in face of the snow-capped mountains and accept defeat.

Drenched from head to toe, I embraced the storm as I marched up the main road toward Upper Hutt, knowing it would all pass and the feelings of today would become the struggles of yesterday. But if yesterday's struggles dealt me the feelings of today, then the struggles of today would sculpt the will of tomorrow. Did that mean my will would forever be tainted by yesterday's storm?

In spite of the dark clouds forming in my mind I knew I was going to be okay, at least in the end—if this journey had an end. The fog blanketed the weary northern roads, making any type of future seem uncertain—however I knew I would get somewhere, for my will was yet to break. As long as I was here, on this road, with my vision clasped between my hands, I could only move forward, not back.

Chapter 4

Night fell upon me, the air sharp and crisp against my face. It was a nice change from the soaring coastal gusts, yet still, I had to wrestle with the bone shattering breeze sweeping over the valley from the mountain tops. The town sparkled in the distance, meaning only one thing, food. On the main strip there would be an abundance of takeaway shops, out back the bins would be steaming with burgers, pizza… whatever didn't quite make it into the hands of *hungry* people.

My head felt heavy. My legs cramped up and I couldn't hold my focus any longer than ten seconds. Either way, I was fatigued or developing the flu. To minimize the distance between myself and the town, I veered off the main road taking a short cut through the suburbs. Six o' clock dinners filled the airways seeping into my nostrils to the point of tasting what was being cooked on my tongue. Slow cooked beef… potatoes… steamed vegetables… Instead of following the road into town, I followed my nose and got lost deeper in the suburbs, finding myself in a place called Shakespeare Avenue.

I stared into the light of someone's kitchen window. A guy with black rimmed glasses and a woolly beard stood over a frying pan. He must've just knocked off work because he was still dressed in a stone-grey button up shirt, tucked into navy blue trousers. I watched him flip his steak, hearing the meat sizzle in the pan. I drooled out the corner of my mouth.

Thunder rumbled in the skies, filling up the valley like a thousand hands clapping in applause. The guy in the kitchen jolted in fright, he leaned over the kitchen sink to peer out the window, expecting to see the thunder bolts Zeus threw down at us, but instead, he met eyes with a weary bum who looked like he had been swimming all day.

He turned off the element and rushed down the hall. *Great*, I thought, *there you go again, Corey, sitting outside people's houses like a hungry dog waiting to be fed.*

The front door creaked open ajar. 'Can I help you?' the guy asked shakily. I could see the fear forming in his eyes. The last thing I wanted was to cause anybody distress, but how does one justify himself given my circumstance? *Don't mind me, I'm just admiring those magical smells wafting out your kitchen...* That'd be weird. He'd just throw me in the category of straightjackets and soft white walls.

'Sorry to bother you, I just haven't eaten much today,' I explained. 'I was supposed to be heading into town but found myself lured in by your cooking.'

A lady with dark hair and glasses and a book in hand, popped her head out the door. 'Tom,' she said, 'is everything okay out here?'

He took a while to answer, startled by the unlikelihood of the situation. 'Yeah, everything's fine, honey. Someone's just hungry…'

She gazed at me warily before retreating to the warmth of their fireplace.

'I'll be on my way,' I said. 'Sorry to creep you out—'

'No wait,' he said. 'Where is it you were heading?'

'Just into town,' I replied. 'Maybe I'll find shelter at Maidstone Park.'

He shook his head slowly, as if having trouble processing what I said. 'Hang on a sec, I've got some food you can take with you.' He closed the door and locked it. A few moments later he came back with a pile of tinned food. His wife held the door open for him and he placed the tins of food on the porch at a safe distance, as if I were some stray human who was prone to attack. I didn't blame him. If a dripping wet vagrant rocked up to my door at dinner time, I'd probably send him on his way with an empty stomach.

'Can you carry all of it?' he asked. 'Need a plastic bag?'

I stuffed the tins of food into my backpack which was bursting at the seams. 'I might need a plastic bag for the last of it,' I said, smiling apologetically.

His wife came back with a plastic bag, once again, dropping it 1.5 meters away from me. I threw my pack over my shoulders, the weight throwing me off balance. I cracked open a can of pineapples and sculled back the juice. 'Words can't express how grateful I am right now,' I said, wiping the juice off my beard.

'No worries, man,' said the guy. 'Stay safe, aye. Best you find some shelter, the storm is sticking around for the rest of the week.'

I nodded, catching one last glimpse at their shock filled faces before giving them a wave as I fled toward the bright lights of town.

***

My pack felt like it was filled with rocks. My scrawny upper body wasn't built to carry anything other than a sack of clothes and a few cans of baked beans. I chugged back the pineapple juice and chewed up the chunks as I walked past a sleazy bar with cheap neon lights flashing like a strobe light if you were stupid enough to stare at it for too long. I released a full-bodied sigh as I finally stepped into the shelter of the long, narrow shopping strip.

There wasn't too much happening in town, at this hour most of the shops were closed. Asides from a few stingy bars housing a handful of lonely drunks and sad eyed people with nothing more than the company of half a beer, I was alone. The streets were so quiet I could hear the train galloping along the tracks a few blocks down. The moon and stars decided to creep out of the gloom, momentarily lighting up the sky, giving vague illuminations to what, or who, was lurking in the shadows.

I followed the dim lights on Main Street, absorbing the points of interest. On the corner there was Al's Pizzeria, half a block down was a McDonald's open 24/7, back the way I came was a Turkish takeaway, not to mention all the fish and chip shops that seemed to spawn on every street corner like a rash. But every one of them would prove to be useless. I had no trouble dumpster-diving in the city, pickings were never slim, a larger population meant it was harder to regulate. But in Upper Hutt, all the goddamn bins had thick chains and heavy padlocks strapped around them.

My initial thoughts were to beat the crap out of the bin in a fit of rage until it cracked and pillage the bins like a westernized takeover. I wondered why there were locks on the bins in the first place, when they were destined to be taken to the dump, anyway.

The cans of food in my pack quickly became my livelihood. A guaranteed meal. I didn't want to jeopardize my food source by being overly generous to my stomach, the tinned goods were better left preserved, like an emergency resource. However, the weight was a bit too much to bear, so I decided to eat like a king until tomorrow and loosen up the base weight.

Outside the public library, I hid in the shadows and peeled off my wet clothes. Rolling them up, I strained out the water and hung my overcoat and jeans on the hand railing to dry before I hit the streets to find a place to rest my head.

A grandfather clock mounted on the roof of the library read half past ten. It felt like half past ten, there was a nasty chill in the air which stabbed into my skin like a plague of frozen knives. At last, the rain subsided, giving me a moment to catch my breath before I endured yet another drowning. I was unsure of how long my window in the clouds would be open, after watching my clothes drip onto the pavement for ten minutes, dancing around in nothing but my undies to stay warm, I decided to get a move on for the sake of generating body heat.

At this hour, I had to have my wits. This was the hour when the forces of the Yin and Yang really threw everything it could at you. I staggered back to the main drag, feeling like a lost child who somehow separated from the herd. Upper Hutt Central wasn't the most hospitable environment for someone without a home or a safety net to fall back on. It was full of thieves, junkies, prostitutes, and boy-racers who wore the mask of a Greek demigod—that is when they were strapped into the driver's seat with a dumb drunken blonde chick whooping from the backseat. But without their vehicles to reinforce their ego, they looked just as defenceless and pathetic as a mouse trapped inside an enclosure full of lions. Put aside the boy-racers' constant grapple for attention, the real cretins you had to watch out for were the ones hiding in the shadows of park trees and shady alleys, they are the people who wouldn't think twice about ending your life over five bucks in cash and half a packet of cigarettes.

When I was a teenager, I remember seeing some guy

rob a kid for his bike at Maidstone park on a Friday night. The kid didn't put up much of a fight, or at least show the slightest sign of resistance. He just handed over his bike to the guy like it was always his to begin with. The act within itself sickened me. A guy in his twenties pushing around a kid not even half his age. I had to get involved and teach the punk a lesson. I broadened my shoulders, puffed out my chest, and marched toward him. It was then, I saw why the kid handed his bike over so freely. My purposeful strides dismantled, and my legs turned to jelly. I saw it glisten in the moonlight, sparkling in a mystifying manner, as if it were a tool to decide who lived, and who died. He locked eyes with me. I halted, hypnotized by the moonlight gliding along the blade.

'Don't move another fuckin inch!' he demanded.

I didn't object.

Keeping a close eye on me, he hopped onto the bike, and pedalled into the mist of the autumn night. The kid was left in tears, not only because his bike was stolen, but because he would be stamped on the head with a future diagnosis of post-traumatic stress disorder.

I wondered what kind of hoodlums I'd encounter tonight, or worse, what creatures were already stalking me as I ignorantly roamed the streets, seeing no more than my own wants and selfish needs. Now, that's what catches people off guard, that's what gets people killed.

What kind of parasites wished to leech off me tonight? The corporate tit was never enough, so the phantoms of the night fed on nobodies like me. Let's be real, what repercussions would come their way after desecrating a hobo's front teeth? None. As far as they are concerned, if you've got nowhere to go and you're out on the streets at ungodly hours of the night, you're a bad apple who needs to be turfed.

Behind Queens Plaza, over a rickety barb wire fence—where portions of the fence had been clipped with wire-cutters from top to bottom—was where an old generator from a warehouse pumped out hot air. If you were small enough (like me) you could squeeze through the clipping at the bottom. If you were on the bigger side, you'd have to climb it and hope you didn't get caught in the steel spider's web.

Come winter, it was the equivalent of a holiday away from the cold on evenings like this. But ever since they installed cameras around the joint, security started harassing the homeless and the misfits inevitably cleared out. Desperate times called for desperate measures. How I saw it, I had my own personal dryer—and even better, it was free. Even if security decided to put down their bowl of popcorn and shut down their CCTV screens, I'd be out of there before they lifted themselves off their seats.

Every hobo who was pushed north used to travel here to warm up their bones by the factory generator. Back in the city, when we would hover around burning park bins on winter nights, Homeless Harry used to ramble on about what he called "hobo folklore". He squatted and bludged off too many communities to count and knew enough about tramping around Wellington to write a book. Homeless Harry spoke profoundly about the bitter sweetness of Upper Hutt. The bitterness sprang from the town being built at the foot of a mountain range, and the sweetness was this warehouse generator, which to Harry, was like what a stupa would be to a Buddhist.

Homeless Harry journeyed to and from the generator every winter in the same way a pilgrim would pay homage to Santiago. Unfortunately, Homeless Harry didn't quite reach his "Mecca" ever again. His legs didn't work the way they used to, and he couldn't outrun security. He had been around the block too many times to count and built a name for himself in the Wellington region and abroad. The cops locked him up for public indecency and drunk and disorderly behaviour, despite Harry being sober for almost ten years. They even confiscated his saxophone, claiming it was an "annoyance to the public", even though Homeless Harry made roughly what someone would make on a day's minimum wage by playing in the streets.

If you asked me, it was a bit of a conspiracy, the council didn't want a hobo freeloading whilst getting paid to do so. I'll tell you, the real reason why Homeless Harry made so much money a day blowing into his sax was because he blew heart, character, and soul. The notes he blew reflected the sorrowful streets, the bleakness of contemporary life, and the tender sounds of our hearts breaking in two. Then again, I guess he had little to complain about, at least he didn't have to worry about having a roof over his head at the time.

Once my clothes were dryer than a west Australian

summers day, I decided to vacate the premises. After my ordeal with security earlier in the afternoon, my face would be a photocopied target in and around Upper Hutt. Treading cautiously on the sidewalk, keeping an eye out for any sudden movements, I continued my search for a safe place to sleep. Then, suddenly it hit me in the face like a savage uppercut. Somehow, the tone of the town turned ugly. I don't know how or why, but there was an air of depravity, it was sinful and wicked, a feeling I still struggle to describe. All I heard around me was the groaning car engines of boy-racers, it consumed every inch of space. I felt surrounded and outnumbered. They pushed their mechanical beasts to its limits, lashing it on the back through each lacerating shift in gear. Just when I thought my head was going to explode, my ears popped. The noise pollution dissipated. I sighed, my heart beating rapidly.

Was I caught in the middle of some twisted dream? I sort of lost myself for a moment. But then I remembered where I was and what time it was. I wrapped around the corner, getting goosebumps at the thought of someone stalking me.

A black car appeared, the engine was running, and the lights were on. The man in the car appeared to be waiting for someone—or more so an opportunity. He rolled down his window as I passed. 'Hey kid,' he said. 'Wanna make some money?'

He was no longer an elusive shadow, I could see his face, his demeanour, his intentions. He was dressed tidily, passing off as a respectable working-class citizen who didn't quite *make it* in the eyes of the world—not to say he *didn't* make it—but that didn't go without bending, reshaping, and reforming his persona to better suit the pleasing eyes of the system.

'Not interested,' I replied, shuffling past him without a further glance.

'Come on,' he implored, waving his hand insistently.

I heard his car door open. I spun around only to witness a sight I wish I could forget—erase. His trousers were around his ankles. He leered at me hungrily as he fondled his erect penis. 'Just a hundred bucks for a minute of your time, pal. Best deal you'll get in this asshole of a town."

I picked up my pace, but the degenerate must've had his hand on the steering wheel as opposed to his cock, and he cruised alongside me with his head hanging out the window. I wish I had Homeless Harry's trusty torch. The bulky thing weighed a kilogram without batteries. It was steel framed and rigid enough to crack skulls. I foolishly lost it after getting lucky one Tuesday night on Queens Wharf—or rather the chick I got with swiped it along with a thread from my coat and some pocket lint.

As I considered the notion of sprinting for the nearest alleyway, he continued to stalk me, blurting out obscenities like, 'You're not gonna get away that easy! I know boys who'd give an arm to have an offer like that, just stick your tongue down my throat for a fifty!' He became erratic and had the look of a man who should be locked away for good. 'Just get in the goddamn car!' he snapped. 'Don't make me drag you in by your ankles!'

'Fuck off!' I shouted, hoping to alarm somebody—anybody, so they knew I was being harassed by some chump who jacked off into Kleenex tissues in late night parking bays. Of course, there was no one around. Often in times of crisis there never really was anybody around—at least no helping hands reached out to me when I was in need—maybe because I didn't pay my taxes, and technically speaking I wasn't an *actual* citizen. A human, yes, but a registered one? Let's just say I threw away my collar.

But life's full of surprises, even if the surprise was a bunch of rotten punks with a baseball bat in hand, taking wild swings at a sexual predator's wagon. Wait a second. I had to look twice to believe it. An old 80s model car swerved around violently with a bald-headed boy hanging out the backseat window. He had a reckless glimmer in his eyes. The boy gripped the baseball bat tightly, lining up his next shot which happened to be the sleaze bags face. He seemed to be familiar with the potential paedophile and yelled out all types of threats at him. 'If I see your face around town again—you better pray I don't…Four traumatized horses at the Silverstream stables… you sick fuck… we know what you did… I'll castrate you with my bare hands, Wesley!'

The bald-headed juvenile's words must have struck a chord within him because the sex-pest put his foot down and raced off in the direction of the highway. I needed to get away from the madness, find a peaceful patch of grass to sleep on, and more importantly, get the hell away from Upper Hutt Central.

In this moment I decided to leave Upper Hutt first thing tomorrow morning, if this was the kind of grit that drifted in the town, I wanted no part in it. I'd place my trust in following the free-flowing rivers upstream.

The old car pulled in beside me. 'You all right?' asked the bald-headed juvenile. He smiled, revealing a mouthful of missing teeth. Then the driver said, 'You headin' anywhere in particular? I can give ya a ride if ye want.'

I contemplated his offer.

He sensed my ambivalence and said, 'No pressure. Just thought you looked like you needed a hand, that's all. The name's Clinton, if it means anythin' to y'all.' Half a shadow cast over his face, but I could see enough of him to know he was good looking in an abstract kind of way, his eyes were big and dreamy—probably from all the dope he smoked—his hair brown and wayward, sticking up in different places, yet it worked and somehow looked almost like he styled it. He had a strong southern accent, like he was brought up on a farm in Ashburton or somewhere around Canterbury.

The other two guys looked like trouble. The bald-headed juvenile gripping the baseball bat had the look of a kid who had been through the system numerous times, Residents, foster homes—the system had failed him to say the least. The other guy who was in the front seat remained quiet—too quiet for my liking. Clinton told me his name was Anthony. He was in his mid-twenties and had a scar running across one eye. He had the look of a guy who wanted to tear the world in half for no other reason than for his own amusement.

I had nowhere else to go, plus, the heat from the car was already warming up my blood, so I hopped in the back door—in which the kid held open for me. I couldn't help but feel I made the wrong choice, either way, it didn't matter because like the door, any other options were now closed.

They glared at me like I was some alien they just picked up off the side of the road. The silence was killing me. I had to avert their attention, their eyes drilled deep into my exterior, making me feel like they were psychically attacking me. I had to say something to break the ice, anything. 'Fresh out of Residents, aye?' I said to the youngster.

My statement seemed to rub him the wrong way, his face turned foul—if it could get any more offensive— and he grounded what was left of his teeth. I should have just kept my mouth shut. I was so socially deprived I lost all my communication skills, not that they were the best to begin with.

The driver, Clinton, interjected before things got too heated. He looked me dead in the eye and said, 'We're cruisin' around for a bit, you're welcome to join—guess it's warmer in here than it is outside, aye.' He gestured to the dull black sky.

'Yeah,' I agreed, relaxing into my seat as he took off and spun around the roundabout, leaving the town to wallow in its own misery.

Chapter 5

We drove in silence all the way to Timberlea. Clinton made a couple of pit stops along the way. Strangers stepped out of the shadows and made their way over to his car. He shook many hands and like a magician, money appeared in his hands once the deal was done. He then steered his wagon into a long, steep driveway with large overhanging ferns reminding me of an earthy rooftop.

'Wait in here,' he said, slamming the door.

He hurried up the concrete staircase to the front door. As he climbed the stairs, he set off the security lights which shed light on tall Nikau palms growing on the banks surrounding the house. The lights trickled over the fronds of the palm, which moved sluggishly in the breeze as if it were burnt out and tired.

A hooded man answered, he clapped Clinton's hand, and pulled him in for half a hug. Clinton then jogged down the stairs and back to the car. He threw a small bag of weed at Blaze (the bald-headed juvenile, apparently after years of Residents and countless social worker meetings you can choose your own name).

'Roll us up a fat one, Blaze,' said Clinton, 'with a bit of tobacco, I wanna at least save half of it for another one later.'

'Sweet as,' Blaze replied, pulling a breadboard out of the backrest, laying it down on his lap, just in case he dropped any crumbs. From out of his military styled khaki pants, he pulled out a grinder and a packet of extra-large rolling papers. He tore off a bit of cardboard from the back, rolling the cardboard into a filter tip.

Impressed, I watched him methodically carry out the procedure he clearly had down to an art form. Blaze expertly dampened the sticky tab, sealing the joint off with a bit of himself in order to complete the ritual. What amazed me the most was while Blaze was doing all of this, Clinton was reversing down the long and winding driveway like a maniac, and Blaze still managed to pull off something that would be noteworthy in Amsterdam's wall of fame.

'The roller has the honours,' said Clinton.

Blaze sparked up and puffed on the thing like a steam train. He inhaled more than he could handle and spurted out a cloud of smoke while exploding into coughing fits. I half smiled. In the back of my mind, I knew he was trying to make a statement for himself, I'd seen it all before when I was his age. There's nothing more dangerous than a teenager hanging out with a bunch of older guys or girls, they'll go to extreme lengths only to impress those who really don't give a rats ass to begin with. But it doesn't stop them from trying, again and again, until they land in jail for aggravated assault charges—or worse, when they revert to hanging out with punks who are their own age, they think it gives them some sort of Charlie Manson pack leader quality, which again, leads naive youth down a destructive avenue. I gazed at Blaze, my smile growing broader. He was an easy read, like a young adult novel. *Teenagers can be so dumb*, I thought. If only they could see themselves for what they are, then they'll realize what they're worth.

Clinton tore the joint out of Blaze's hand and took his time with it, the joint appeared to be in safer hands. He then passed it to Anthony. He took deep, glum drags and became even quieter than he was before—if it was at all possible. Eventually the joint came around to me. Now, I stopped smoking years ago, for reasons as simple as it didn't do what it used to do for me, sort of like a girlfriend until they became an ex.

Anthony shuffled around in the front seat, he mumbled something, but I didn't interpret it to be English. He then handed me what was pretty much the roach of the joint—Clinton did go to town on the thing. I felt the hazy eyes of the others stabbing into me, come to think about it, they were all starting to look Chinese. I knew exactly what was going down. A man (or woman) is judged upon how they handle the buzz and their ability (or lack of) to gel into the vibrations of the group. It practically determined whether you were "one of them". Every move I made in this moment was pivotal—that is, if I were playing their game.

'What the hell are you waiting for, Corey!' Clinton grumbled, fiendishly glaring at the roach. 'It's burning out for Christ sake!'

Of course, this set off Blaze and he too started winging about how he would have finished it by now. Immediately I regretted getting into the car. I just wanted to find a quiet alley with some shelter, a place that repulsed people so I knew I would be left alone. As for now, I was stuck with three dope fiends who shoved their insecurities in my face and claimed they were my own.

What to do? I thought. If you can't beat em, join em… what a cop out, though. *Uh, what the hell, maybe one puff will shut them up.*

I placed the roach to my lips and took a polite drag.

'There,' I said. 'You happy?'

Blaze chuckled out loud, displaying his amusement to the others. 'You smoke like a bitch!' he said.

Oh, here we go, I thought, he's found his moment to strike.

It was then I felt a warm bundle of euphoria creep up my spine. It eased the anxious tension pulsating through my muscles, as if an angel rested her healing hands on my shoulders. Where did these feelings come from? It happened so fast, this sudden snap in perception which had me feeling like I was a direct plug-in to the stimulus contained within matter. Everything that once was, "I think", became "I feel". Only a second ago I was perched on my high horse, categorically judging Blaze and his blind foolishness, and then I met eyes with the

50

inexplicable. I understood why he changed his name. He wanted to sever all ties to his past, maybe it was an abusive one, maybe it was filled with poverty. My previous judgments were just as foolish as the box I threw him into.

Just as I thought things couldn't get any more bizarre, I fell through another layer of myself. I saw Homeless Harry blowing into his saxophone, standing before the grand pillars outside the Wellington train station, drawing upon the commuters repressed emotions. He was like a gardener of the mind, each note he blew he pulled out weeds, freeing up space so happiness could fill up the holes and cracks in people's lives.

Blowing his saddest, most beautiful note, he met eyes with me. He smiled; I saw nothing but the smiling faces of other people reflecting through his reflective glasses. Though, I noticed something offbeat was dancing behind him, something that didn't quite blend into his blues. It was a gloomy apparition. The beast was transparent, as if present in two dimensions at once. It dug its claws into homeless Harry's shoulders and pulled him back until he lost his footing. Homeless Harry slipped through the cracks in the pavement, becoming one with the spit and other types of pavement scum. His saxophone sort of hovered in mid-air, then suddenly it dropped to the sidewalk, shattering into a million pieces. Wellington city turned cold; everything went dark…

'He's fuckin greening out!' Blaze shouted. He was all strung out and excited like a kid at a mate's place for a sleepover. He shook me by my shoulders, laughing hysterically.

'Get the fuck off me!' I demanded, my eyes darting around the interior of the car, desperately trying to find my grip on reality.

'Take it easy now, princess,' Blaze said, easing up on me.

The car wasn't moving. Clinton must have pulled over when he realized I was dead to the world.

'What's in this thing?' I asked, demanding an explanation for the *big bang* that went off inside my head.

Clinton leaned in close and said in his tangy, country-boy accent, 'Let's just say some fairies grew fond of us, and they sprinkled some of their fairy dust on our smoke—'

'You fuckin drugged me!'

'Not exactly,' Clinton broke in, 'we didn't hold the joint to your lips and force it down your throat—we could of... we could of done a lot of things to you, if we really wanted...'

The gig was up. It was official, I had been lured into the serpent's nest. Whatever was in the joint still had me pinned down to my seat, making any ideas of sudden movement impossible. In order to move my arm, I had to verbally instruct my body to adhere to my command. I felt completely out of proportion with my body, a giant sitting in a toy sized car. I needed fresh air—open space.

'You okay now, Corey?' asked Clinton casually, not seeming to care I was on the verge of a breakdown. 'Don't you think its 'bout time I get this space craft back in the clouds... what ya say?'

He flicked on his indicator, checked his blindside, and steered the car onto the main road—God only knew how he was still driving. As far as Clinton was concerned it was a car by day, and a space cruiser by night.

The air in the car got stuffy, my skin began to crawl—like actually began to crawl, maybe microscopic insects were crawling all over me—all I was breathing in was the stale cigarette smoke Anthony blew out of his tar-stained lungs. The back window didn't open, either it refused to budge, or my hands were out of sync with my mind, I didn't know. To make matters worse, Blaze rolled up another "elemental joint", Clinton claimed it was the icing on the cake. I don't know what kind of cake Clinton envisioned, but I felt sick to my stomach by the mere thought of another slice. I gave up on trying to open the window and resorted to clawing at it, like an animal held prisoner at the zoo.

'Settle the fuck down!' Blaze grumbled, restraining me with my seatbelt.

'Let me out! I can't breathe in here!'

Clinton caught my eye in the rear-view. 'It's all in your head, man. See, I can breathe just fine…' He took a deep drag on the joint, filling the car up with more smoke.

At this stage, being stuck in the car was worse than Russian torture. I just wanted out, was that too much to ask?

Clinton decided to snap out of his carefree, white trash façade and spoke with the authority of a cop. 'All-right, Corey. This is how it's going to go down. We'll

drop you back into town, under one condition though…'
He looked to his comrades. 'How's that sound boys?' He
peered at Anthony, who gave him a soulless stare, a look
that said he didn't care if they beat me to a pulp and leave
me for dead on the Manawatu gorge.

'I don't think we should let 'em go so easy,' piped
Blaze, sounding like one of those miniature dogs yapping
from the backseat.

'I'll sew that sweet little mouth of yours shut if I have
to!' snapped Anthony.

I was just as shocked as the others to hear Anthony
finally coming out of his shell—or better said, rising out
of his tomb.

'Didn't pass you off as someone who knows how to
sew,' said Clinton, shrugging.

'You know what I fuckin' mean,' replied Anthony.

'Well,' Clinton continued, 'now that we've
established that… let's get back to what I was saying—do
any of you remember what I was saying?'

'You were sayin' 'bout checkin' Corey real good
before we throw him back on the streets,' said Anthony.

Clinton said, 'Anthony, you're a strain on my mind at
times, but you ain't too bad, sorta like a strung-out
receptionist.'

Anthony didn't like the sound of that.

Clinton, once again, started talking like a cop. 'We're
not gonna let you lose in the streets without some kind of
idea of what you're holding.'

'Holding?' I asked.

'Hand over your bag, Blaze needs to sniff out its

contents. Beware, he bites.'

Blaze bared his teeth at me—what was left of them. He snatched my bag which was resting by my feet before I had the time to protest. He pulled it apart, stacking the items into two piles, presumably what was useful and useless to them. He gave Clinton a quick nod, as if to say the going was good, then he packed it up. Instead of handing me back what was rightfully mine, he passed it to Anthony in the front seat, who dropped it between his legs for safe keeping.

'I'm afraid we're gonna have to take this off your hands,' Clinton said gravely. 'Us boys haven't eaten in days, and the rest of the stuff will look pretty damn good in a Cash Converters window, don't ya think?'

'Fuck you!' I managed to blurt out.

'No,' Clinton interjected, 'thank you, Corey. Pleasure doin' business with y'all.'

'Business—'

The car came to a screeching halt outside Al's Pizzeria. I was back at the very start of where all this madness unfolded. Anthony stepped out of the car, he was a lot taller than I anticipated, easily six foot, cold faced, and butt ugly. Clinton flicked off the child-lock on the door, and Anthony swooped on in, roughing me up with his Goliath hands. He grabbed me by the scruff of my neck and hurled me out the car and to the streets like a bag of trash on rubbish day.

It happened all so fast I barely had enough time to feel anything at all. As they raced away and out of sight, leaving me with nothing except for the clothes on my back, I managed to swallow my thumping heart and finally put everything into perspective. Hatred washed over me. I let it surge through my veins trying my best to remain conscious of my emotions, the last thing I wanted was to cause anymore unnecessary drama for myself. I failed in containing my emotions. One lonely tear dribbled down my face, a tear I let slip from my otherwise dried up well of emotions.

I'm okay, I kept telling myself, all will be fine. . . who am I kidding.

I heard the streets of Lower Hutt scream from afar: *"What's mine is mine! What's yours is my desires!"*

Everyone wants to take something from you, there is no such thing as a life without conditions. Whether it's what you take when you go to work, and what work takes from you, your family and friends, the clerk at the liquor store, a trio of thugs—it doesn't matter whether its tangible or intangible, regardless, on the inside people will be rubbing their hands together about it, like vultures circling a dying animal.

So, what would become of me if I stripped myself of all *things*? What would I manifest on this planet? For starters, Clinton, Blaze, and Anthony would cease to exist in my small pocket of the universe. There'd be no backpack, no opportunity, no will to seek. But then what would become of me? Would I be dead to the world, because after all, we only exist in the world of *things*. Uh, I don't care anymore. There were too many questions begging for elaborate answers. It was getting late, my eyes were heavy, soon they'd fall out if I didn't stop rubbing them. We're all doomed from the start anyway. That's a sentiment I could rest my head on until morning.

Chapter 6

Needless to say, I didn't rest my head on my sentiments. After I was thrown back into town, I dragged myself back to the factory generator where I slept for two hours until I was awoken by the headlights of a security vehicle. They shooed me off and I wavered out of town. This place was cursed anyway, everything wished to hinder my progress and for no reason at all, make life difficult.

At around two in the morning, I ventured back to the outskirts of town, retracing my steps to the river's edge. I took my time as I could only see a meter or so in front of me, but this time something wasn't right about the river trail—and it wasn't the fact I was hiking in complete darkness. I felt naked without my pack, like I had nothing to lean on, literally. No longer could I call this an odyssey of some kind, without my pack I was just following lines of dirt.

What is a man without food, shelter, and basic necessity? I thought. A bum. A good for nothing bum. And that's all

I was despite what I hoped to be, but with my backpack strapped around my shoulders, I felt like a *somebody* trekking over the contours of Aotearoa's flesh.

I had no clue where I was heading but followed the river, using the distant lights as a guide. I encountered a bridge linking Upper Hutt Central to Totra Park and decided to curl up in a ball under the bridge and try to get some sleep. However, my stomach refused to let me. I was starving and couldn't get over the fact my one and only food source had been ripped away from me.

I tried to suppress my anguish, the way western society had taught me to do since I was a boy, but these feelings could no longer be bottled or kept in a jar, they had already spilled over the edge and caused a hell of a mess. I needed to eat, and I didn't care how I obtained my food. I'd throw a brick threw some chumps kitchen window and raid his fridge for all I cared.

Using my stomach as a compass, I found myself in some suburb between Upper Hutt and Totra Park. The sounds of thumping bass, accompanied by the ecstatic murmurs of a platoon of drunkards, echoed throughout the streets, like it was the very heartbeat of suburbia. The sounds pulled my head from out of the clouds and back to the scum of pavement. A sharp breeze swept through my overcoat. I pulled up my hood, tightening the drawstrings and buttoned up my coat. The infamous Wellingtonian rain soon came down in buckets.

So much for dry clothes, I thought.

I heard a wailing voice coming from my stomach. I gave it a pat, reassuring it I hadn't forgotten about it. The thumping bass grew louder with every step as I splattered through puddles. I hovered beneath a tortured willow tree growing outside the property where the party was taking place, shielded by a rusted corrugated iron fence. The branches draped over me, providing little coverage, the rigid branches reminded me of the remains of some beast made of bark who endured a slow and painful death.

By now it was 3 A.M., surely, I'd be able to slip in unnoticed, if worse came to worse, I was no novice and had a few tricks up my sleeve, after all, dealing with drunks was like dealing with children—unpredictable and at times violent children.

I peered over the fence, there were two people muttering incoherently with beers held to their chest. Waltzing in through the main entrance was off the cards, so I crawled through some bushy shrubs, making my way around to their backyard. I peeped over the fence, keeping my eyes peeled for a dog kennel, bones, or dog bowls—any give away sign to prevent myself from being torn to shreds.

Over the fence there was nothing but an overgrown patch of grass—a weak excuse for a backyard. There was a small patio, a washing line, and a bunch of bins. I tossed a pebble over the fence, hitting the aluminium roof with a sharp thud. I held my breath, awaiting the snarls of a blood thirsty Rottweiler.

Silence.

I hurdled over the fence, sinking ever so slightly when I landed in the small squishy patch of grass. I leaped out of my skin when I noticed movement by the washing line, though it was only a pair of socks and a rugby jersey pegged to the line.

I proceeded to scout out the backyard searching for any tools to assist me. Firstly, I needed a beer in hand to blend in with the others. I spotted a small bar fridge sitting beside the back door in the patio. I was heading toward the fridge when I noticed her.

Half of a girl sobbed into her hands—the other half of her body resided in the shadows. She rested her back on the washing line post as rain trickled down her exposed shoulders, soaking her little dress that looked too cold for a night like this.

It came as second nature to stop and ask if she was okay. But then my conniving means of survival intercepted my kind, nurturing instinct. I could hear her out, discuss her problems, introduce myself, and gain my right of acceptance among the pack. Soon enough, my belly would be full of steaks, sausages, and whatever sides were lingering about—hell, I may as well drink as many lagers as I could to make the long walk north that much more interesting.

'Excuse me?' I said, careful to not impose. 'Are you okay?'

She jolted frightfully, glancing up at me with watery brown eyes.

'I'm fine,' she said quickly, rising to her feet. She brushed off her skimpy skirt and headed for the back door.

Playing my *angel in the night* role I said, 'Burying the

problem alive will only mean it will return from the dead.'

She spun around. 'Who the fuck do you think you are? My old man or something? Fuck off!' She stormed off toward the back door, then halted in the doorway.

'Hold on,' she muttered. 'Who even are you anyway?'

She put me on the spot unexpectedly—too soon for my liking. I hesitated. My clasp on the situation weakening.

She stepped closer to get a better look. 'I've never seen you at Danny's before.'

'I'm a work mate,' I said quickly.

'Is that so?' she replied. 'Danny hasn't worked for five years...' Refusing to take her eyes off me, she screeched, 'Danny! There's some creep in your backyard who claims he knows you!'

I flirted with the idea of jumping the fence and fleeing there and then. But a staunch Māori man appeared who I assumed to be Danny. He had muscular arms that were both covered in tribal tattoos, within his eyes I saw the look of a reincarnated Māori warrior.

'What's up, cuz?' he said, in a deep ballsy voice.

The girl stood in the light of the patio; she too was Māori. 'This fella just magically appeared in your backyard; he reckons he worked with you—'

'It was a long time ago,' I said. 'You probably don't remember me.'

Danny looked me up and down, his wide crazy eyes protruding out of his swollen eye sockets. 'I don't forget a face, bro, and I'll tell ya, I don't recognize your ugly mug.'

'I must've got the wrong address,' I said soberly, patting my overcoat pockets as if searching for an invitation of some kind.

Tension filled the air. What to do next? Get on one knee and beg for his mercy, or run like the wind and free myself from slaughter.

The girl, I only knew as 'cuz', looked to and from Danny and me, as if expecting a primate to leap out of his skin and bash me to death with his bare hands.

'Look at the state of you,' Danny said finally, gesturing to my saturated coat. 'You must've been standing out here pretty long to be as wet as you are—'

'Danny,' the girl interrupted, 'I didn't see, but I reckon he jumped over the fence, he probably knows about your plants—'

'Shut your fuckin' mouth!' Danny shouted. 'I want facts, not some presumption, Tay.'

So, he was a man of intellect, not a man who used his fists to serve justice.

He turned back to me. 'What's your name?'

My mind ticked. I hesitated a moment too long.

Unimpressed with my lack of an answer, he shook his head. 'You've got ten seconds… ten seconds to run. But I'll find you, I'll hunt you down like a dog hunting a pig!'

Okay, maybe he does dish out justice with his fists. Then it occurred to me, why not have a crack at his mind, I had nothing to lose other than my front teeth.

'I swear, I know you,' I said insistently.

'What's my last name then?'

63

'Amakura,' I said without a lapse in speech.

Both Danny and the girls faces dropped. He flashed a goofy smile, revealing a bunch of missing teeth. 'So that's where the missing pots been going,' he said hysterically. 'It's gone straight to my head!' He unleashed a hearty laugh that came from his gut.

A heavy gust of wind swept through the valley. The rugby jersey and socks on the line flapped wildly as the pegs struggled to hold onto them. I glanced over my shoulder at the rugby jersey that had the number 8 written on the back, above the number it said, "Amakura". I smiled to myself, quietly agreeing with Danny, the pot had gone to his head.

In the cover of the patio, Tay threw a jacket over her sleek cinnamon-coloured shoulders and folded her arms. 'I think you're full of shit,' she said with a whole lot of sass. 'I know you jumped over the fence, plus, Danny only has a handful of pakeha mates...'

Tay's statement provoked Danny's curiosity. 'I can count my pakeha bros on one hand,' he said. 'In order to separate my friends from my enemies, I don't have as many friends as my fingers can count... So, you're sayin' you're a mate of mine but I don't even know your face. Do you know what category that puts you into?'

I shrugged, not wanting to know the answer.

'That makes you an enemy—'

He came at me. Before I knew it, my head was trapped in the vice of Danny's armpit. I tried to free myself but with little avail. The more I resisted the more pressure he put around my neck until my vision started to blur. I stopped resisting and accepted the idea of my death when the back door flung open. Startled, Danny loosened his grip.

A hefty guy wearing a snapback cap with a big beer gut and a round jolly face staggered out the door, juggling half a dozen beers in both hands. He misjudged the final step leading out to the patio and face-planted straight into the concrete. Bottles went airborne and crashed into the concrete like kamikaze beer bottles. He lay on the ground unresponsive for a moment, then sprang to his feet with bits of green glass stuck to his face. He swept the glass off his brow with his fingertips. 'I didn't realize there was a step in my way,' he chuckled. 'My legs didn't listen to me when I warned them about it though and look what happened.' He roared with laughter. 'I crack myself up sometimes, aye. Anyway, cheah the bros, didn't realize the party was out here, aye.'

'Warren,' Danny said. 'Go back inside, you're drunk.'

'I'm not drunk,' Warren protested, as he picked bits of glass out of his teeth. 'I'm just gettin' started.'

Warren met eyes with me. I saw a flicker of familiarity in his sloth-like brown eyes. 'Al, Hambley?' he said to me. 'Nick Hambley, is that you?'

I wriggled around in attempt to loosen Danny's hold on me.

'Danny, why the fuck you got the bro Hambley in a headlock?'

'The bro?' Danny asked.

'Yeah,' replied Warren, slapping Danny's muscular arms. Danny let me go and I dropped to the ground like a deflated chew toy. 'Ease off the buds, cuz,' Warren said. 'Me and Hambley go way back, ain't that right, cuz?'

I gave Warren a convincing nod.

'Chur, Whitieria music, class of 2010—you still pluckin' the bass bro?'

'Yeah,' I said, nodding again, but this time a little less convincing.

'Far,' Warren continued, 'I haven't been back to tech in ages, not since the good old days—you been back bro?'

'Just for graduation,' I replied.

Warren cracked up laughing and punched me in the arm. 'You're still a crack up guy... you graduated, aye?' He chuckled again. 'We flunked out not even halfway through the course. Some things never change, you're still full of shit!' He beamed at me as he popped the cap off a lager which he lifted out of his baggy pockets. 'Far out, you look so different—you look like you need to have a good feed, bro.' He shook his head. 'How long has it been? Must be coming on five years now...'

'Something like that,' I muttered, exchanging glances with Danny and Tay. I couldn't bury my nerves; I was afraid my fear was so obvious even Warren in his inebriated state would notice it.

'Bro, you're wasted,' Tay said to Warren. 'Right now, you couldn't tell the difference between a fork and a spoon, so what makes you think you know this pakeha fella—they all look the same some way or another.'

I wondered if I should be offended by Tay's statement. But instead brushed it off and stuck close to

Warren, he seemed to be my ticket to safety. The only problem that made me nervous was whether Warren would sober up, it was unclear to me what drugs he ingested to make him believe I was this, *Nick Hambley* guy. The other thing was not knowing what time he started drinking heavily—all this aside, I had to keep feeding him whatever beers were available so he would continue to believe I was his mate from music school.

Warren made a mouth gesture with his hand and said to Tay, 'Blah blah blah… That's all I hear come out of your mouth. I don't get your *mumbo jumbo*. There's no need to be a bitch just cos you got rejected by Tama.'

'Not even,' Tay protested. 'He's just as disgusting to my eyes as you are.'

Warren uttered another laugh from deep within his belly. 'So, you were having so much fun at the party you thought you'd have a cry in the rain outside?'

Tay folded her arms, her eyes darkening like the skies. She pushed past Warren and rushed back into the house while muttering, 'You stupid fat fuck.'

I glanced at Danny, expecting to see his bullish eyes glowing red. But he appeared to be consumed by Warren and Tay's quarrel, and to my relief temporarily forgot about me.

He barged through Warren as he went after Tay to see if she was okay. Before Danny disappeared inside, he turned back to me and raised his finger at me. 'I'm not done with you.'

Hardly phased, Warren shrugged him off. 'Al, Hambley, don't worry 'bout him, he's on too many drugs to know any different.'

'Yeah,' I agreed, thinking to myself it was quite the contrary.

He gestured to follow him through the back door. On the inside, there were a few stragglers left from the party. Standing in the corner of the kitchen was a Bob Marley lookalike, who was preaching to a couple of younger girls in the corner about some *trippy hippy* stuff. He glanced up at me as I followed Warren into the lounge not giving me any second thoughts, evidently Danny's place would have had all types of oddities pouring in at all hours of the day and night.

Warren dropped on the mustard-coloured couch like he had just been shot in the back. The couches looked like they had been picked up from the Salvation Army for ten bucks a piece. The other couches were a loud red and a calm blue, they were discomforting to the senses. Bob Marley banners were hung proudly on either side of the walls, although I'm sure the only song Danny knew was *Smoke Two Joints*. Empty beer bottles covered the coffee table as well as cigarette butts and roaches that didn't quite make it into the ashtray. I eased myself onto the blue couch, watching the clouds of smoke drift lazily below the ceiling.

Across the lounge, in the same room, was the kitchen (it was one of those open planned living setups), on top of the wood-stained bench was the remnants of the barbecue left out in aluminium trays. Beside the trays was a bowl of untouched coleslaw, a bottle of tomato sauce, and a tower of buttered white bread. I lost all sight momentarily, seeing only a char-grilled steak placed in-between two buttery slices of bread, finely salted and topped off with cracked pepper, then with a finishing touch of tomato sauce.

'You hungry bro?' asked Warren, as if he heard my thoughts. 'Get yourself a feed, cuz.'

'Oh, yeah, I could eat,' I said, in a manner which suggested I ate three meals a day. I went straight for the steaks and bread just as Danny came out of the bedroom door.

'What do you think you're doing?' he yelled.

I told him about the sandwich I wished to create.

'That food's for guests,' he said, 'this ain't the Salvation Army bro!'

I was drawn to the size of Danny's fists. They were bigger than my head. Like a child standing behind his father for protection, I fled to the safety of Warren's side, at least then, Danny had a wall of blubber to get through before he got to me.

'Leave him alone, bro,' said Warren sluggishly. He raised an eyebrow and fished out two warm lagers from those baggy pockets of his. He forced one into my hands. 'Drink up, Hambley, life's too short for a man to be without a beer.' He pressed the bottle to his blubbery lips, and just like that, the entire beer vanished down his throat in one effortless gulp. He slipped his hand into his other baggy denim pocket, pulling out another green bottle. I watched on, stunned into a state of amazement and horror. He then dug his hand back into the same pocket, this time fetching half a bag of weed, a lighter, rolling papers, and for some strange reason a small wheel of Brie cheese. I could only assume it was a treat for after his smoke.

'What else you got in there?' I asked. 'By chance, two tickets to a palm riddled paradise?'

Warrens full bellied laugh filled the entire flat. 'Oh, the bro. . .' he said, shaking his head. 'If only I could pull out two big and busty Polynesian girls with flowers in their hair from out of my pocket for you and me… and we'll drink pineapple juice with vodka until we're sick out our ears.'

'Christ, that's quite some vision,' I said, taking a swig of beer. 'About the drinking until I bleed out my ears or something.'

'You've always been a light weight, bro,' Warren said. 'But you're all-good, cuz. Take your time with your beer.'

I liked him. From the moment I met Warren—or more so watched him tumble to the ground like a drunken Sumo—he had this lightness about his presence, like you were free to speak of the most absurd, ridiculous things that came to mind, and he wouldn't judge, or hold it against you. I wanted to tell him then and there I wasn't Nick Hambley, and introduce myself for who I am. That way, I wouldn't be just another face stored in his memory bank, but a *real* friend from a crazy time, a crazy place in our lives. Though I couldn't bring myself to the truth. Not yet at least.

Quite like Blaze did, Warren rolled up a flawless piece of art in spite of seeing possibly two or three of everything. Tay appeared from out of the bedroom, and the Bob Marley lookalike—along with his followers—sat on the opposing couches. Was there something I wasn't hearing? Did Warren pull a little bell out from his plenty-full pockets and give it a ring to let everyone know it was 4:20? Or did this Bob Marley lookalike teach everybody how to awaken their socio-psychic link?

My teeth started to chatter, and I couldn't keep my leg from shaking like it wanted to get up and away from this ritualistic gathering. I twiddled my thumbs as I was consumed by the traumatic flashbacks from the last time I came together with a group of strangers.

Tay held a flame out to Warren and before I knew it, the joint was being passed to the left. Not too long after, everyone's eyes turned red and puffy, kind of like they had just woken up and were ready to put on a pot of morning coffee.

'Save someathat for Hambley,' Warren said to Danny. 'The bro will go up in flames if you leave him a measly puff.'

'Go ahead,' I said quickly, 'don't let me hold things up.'

Warren glared at me sourly and said, 'What're you talkin' bout? If there's anyone here who appreciates a good sesh, it's you. Go on.' Warren encouraged.

Dumbfounded, I stared back at him, the smoke was pouring off the joint like a waterfall in reverse. Warren and the others seemed incredibly stressed by this occurrence. I refused to dance around the dilemma, so I told him the truth, well, half of the truth. 'I'm done with weed,' I said. 'Turns my friends into strangers, turns me against myself.'

Warren eyed me like I had just slapped him in the face. He blinked excessively, struggling to process my honesty. I gazed back at him unflinchingly, expecting the worst, yet content with the cyclone of fists heading my way.

'But you smoke every day,' he said. 'Back at course you were flickin' buds off to everyone, your old man grows—'

'He's a phony,' Tay blurted, flipping her phone around to Warren. He snatched it out of her hands, closing one eye, slightly tilting his head to make sense of the three phone screens he was seeing. It was the Facebook Upper Hutt community page. A CCTV image of me crouching beside the factory generator and meeting eyes with the camera, had been posted by Impenetrable Security Upper Hutt, along with a paragraph summing up how I was "dangerous" and had no regard for the law, informing the community to "keep a look out for this scumbag" and something about keeping your doors locked. The CCTV cameras must have endured some facial recognition process, because below the brief summary of my infringements was my name. If I didn't already feel naked without my pack, now I felt like my skin had been peeled off and my organs were on display to the world.

Warren continued to stare blankly at the post on Tay's phone, as if struggling to gain a grasp of what was going on.

'He's not Nick Hambley you fuckin' idiot!' Tay

shouted, snatching her phone off him and reciting the paragraph, in which he probably couldn't read. The entire time he was more than likely trying to make sense of the image, wondering why Tay showed a picture of me crouched beside a factory generator in the first place.

Warren did what any disgruntled drunk would do given his circumstance, explode in a fit of rage. 'You sonofabitch!' he grunted, attempting to pull his 200-kilogram body off the couch. He fell back into the couch like a toddler learning how to walk, hurling abuse at me like, 'I'll hang you by your balls. You cracker bastard. Crawl back in your mama's womb, you'll be safer in there.'

He was so erratic even Danny had to hold him down. After many failed attempts, Warren managed to pull Danny off him. He lifted the coffee table and savagely threw it at the wall, smashing beer bottles all over the peace symbol on the Bob Marley banner. I slowly backed away, careful to not make any sudden movements, the way one would act around a feral animal.

'You're a fuckin liar!' he shouted. But instead of charging at me like a bull, he broke down and sobbed into his hands. Surprisingly enough, Tay put an arm around him and started stroking his back. Everything about this scene was maddening. I was somewhat sober but felt like I was losing the plot, or the plot had been lost long ago. I started to back away toward a nearby window.

'Where do you think you're going?' Danny yelled. 'You're practically asking to have your head chopped of right now, boy!'

'I can explain!' I begged.

'Ain't no time for that,' he said, 'I'm gonna fuckin' lynch you!' He grabbed a leg piece from the broken coffee table and edged closer to me.

I needed a diversion, anything to distract them long enough so I could make a dash for the nearest exit. It was then I remembered about my wallet, a flimsy cheap leather wallet I picked up outside a bus shelter in the city. Clinton and his pack of apes had robbed me for everything I own, but this wallet had been tucked away snuggly in my pocket the entire time. I fished it out, raised it above my shoulder and threw it in the centre of the lounge where it landed at everyone's feet.

'What the fuck is that?' said Danny, staring at the wallet.

'Take it,' I said, 'there's money in it—it's yours.'

He picked it up to check it out. It gave me enough time to sprint to the back door and out through the patio. I climbed over the corrugated iron fence, slicing my wrist on the rusted edge as I hurdled myself over.

Behind me I heard Danny scream, 'There's nothing fucking in there!'

I knew I was at a safe distance but kept on running just to be certain. I stopped to catch my breath for a couple of seconds, kneeling behind some hedges caught within the shadows of dawn. Panting, I thought to myself, no more Danny, no more Warren or Tay.

My stomach grumbled.

… and of course, still no food.

Chapter 7

The sun was beginning to rise when I crossed the same bridge I tried to sleep under hours before the altercation at Danny's. The sun granted the clarity of sight, illuminating all the darkened corners of my mind I thought I had forgotten. The morning rays revealed a road I used to walk down to get to an old friends place who lived on the other side of the bridge. Her name was Joanna.

I hadn't seen her in years. We never really had a solid friendship to begin with, our binding factor as friends was a shared desire to get high, nothing more. Inevitably, we drifted apart, like debris floating downstream, I floated down the river and got lost in open water, whereas she got stuck in-between some rocks and eventually was pushed to the side of the riverbank, left to float in motionless water, as the stream of life rushed by her side, but never through her.

But there had to be something gluing us together. At

the time I was unaware of it, partly because I was young and too enthralled by the moment to give the time to reflect. Everything was crisp and new back then with something to discover around every corner. But as the years piled on top of me, I could see the binding factor to our friendship. We were both silently miserable, suppressing ourselves with what little we had, sweeping our burdens beneath an unconscious rug.

Joanna had long, curly brown hair with these dark, thick eyebrows she was often teased about—behind her back of course, she gave away too much for people to speak illy to her face. Behind her sad brown eyes, she had the look of someone who was looking out of a steel barred window as the other kids played. One side of her wanted to join the others, meanwhile another wanted to be left alone out of fear of being ridiculed by the pack.

What I found interesting about Joanna was this string of obscure patterns repeating itself like a humourless sitcom. For example, she wasn't attractive, and she wasn't ugly, she wasn't chubby, and she wasn't quite slim, either. Everything about her physical make-up reflected the essence of who she was. Indifferent, mutual, bland, with a little bit of flavour, but not enough to drive you to second helpings. Because she so desperately put herself out there—and let you take as much as you wanted—people stuck around, for all the wrong reasons.

She took on the street kids like they were stray puppies, accommodating their every need in hope of receiving the affection she was without. I met her through some friends who said she pretty much handed out weed and begged you to smoke it.

Both boys and older men had an affinity with Joanna. She built up quite the reputation for sleeping with, well, just about anyone. Teenage boys acquainted themselves with her so they could shamelessly lose their virginities and get a bit of practice in while they were there. As for the older guys—or better said, spineless junkies, being an old drug addict meant you didn't have too many options, so they stuck it where they could.

As for myself, I tolerated her random outbursts and manic episodes, along with all kinds of other attention seeking behaviours, but I didn't stay at her place to get laid. I had my own issues going on at the time. After my old man drank so much, he almost drowned in alcohol, Joanna's was a safe place to put up my feet and get comfortable.

I cut across the rugby field in Totra Park, wondering what day it was. Now I was deep within the suburbs I could barely tell the difference between each day. The city was self-explanatory, and the days revealed itself through everyone's routine. But as for the suburbs, I thought it was a Friday due to the number of parties and heavy drinking on every street corner. What made me clammy and slightly nauseous was the fact the drinking didn't stop. So I knew I landed somewhere in the lower socio-economic grid lines where their weekends began on DOL day, and ended in the cells come Friday.

I separated the wonky piece of timber on Joanna's back fence leading into her backyard (her house backed onto the park). I squeezed in between the weathered timber like I used to do any other time I made unannounced visits. I stared up at the skies backing onto the misty hilltops, based upon the splashes of sunburst peach along with the gentle dissipating blackness, it had to be 6.A.M. This meant I would have to tread carefully; her old man would be putting on a pot of coffee and getting ready to head out the door to work real soon.

Joanna lived in a sleep-out detached from her parents' house. Her curtains were left open as the morning sun crept through the glass sliding door. I was eager to get inside and throw a blanket over my head for the rest of the day. It was so cold outside the grass on the rugby field had frozen over. Every breath I took I exhaled a chilling fog which forced my hands together.

Through Joanna's window I could see two naked, intertwined bodies with blankets tangled around their ankles. It must've been warm in there. I tapped on the sliding door with just enough force to provoke Joanna's attention. She barely shuddered, and rolled over, burying her face in the guy's armpit. I cursed, constantly scanning back and forth to her parents' house, on the lookout for any sudden movements. If her dad decided to take out the rubbish before work, I'd be instantaneously screwed, and back to the cold I march with the cops on my tail.

Again, I peered through the fogged-up glass, wiping it numerous times with my shirt sleeve. Joanna was cuddled up with some dude who had his face buried in the pillow. Her plump pale thigh rested on the side of his buttocks, she spooned him with her face immersed in his bushy ginger hair.

I whacked on the glass with my knuckles. Joanna jolted out of her dreams, she glanced at her boy-toy, but he was still snoring the roof off. Once she caught onto my presence she leaped out of bed, her large breasts jiggled around as she turned the room upside down in hope of finding her dressing gown. At last, she found a blue flannel dressing gown and shamelessly wrapped it around her voluptuous figure. I figured Joanna and her man got too high the night before and couldn't be bothered getting up to close the curtains. She cracked the sliding door open a jar and stared blankly at me without any signs of recognition.

'Joanna,' I said, 'are you going to let me in, or what?'

My voice must have triggered the connection she was looking for because then she said, 'Corey? Corey Gnosis?' My presence seemed to awaken her suddenly. 'What're you doing here?' she murmured, wiping the sleep from her eyes.

'You wouldn't believe me if I told you,' I replied. 'Just let me in. I can explain—I'm freezing my balls off out here.'

No further questions were asked, and she let me in, pulling the curtains closed behind her. On the inside, Joanna's room looked just as chaotic as Danny's place. A heap of condoms had been poured all over the floor beside the bed, one of them was open and looked like they tried to use it, but in the last second discarded the notion of safe sex—either that or the couple of seconds it took to slip into a condom turned the heat of the moment cold.

'Its seven-o-clock in the goddamn morning,' Joanna whispered in a hushed, snappy tone. 'What have you been smoking—if you're on the crack, you've to go—'

'Calm down,' I broke in, 'get me something hot and I'll tell you everything.'

'I'll get you a coffee,' she said sighing. 'My dad should be out the door by now, stay here.' She exited via the sliding door.

'Make that two coffees,' the ginger haired guy murmured drowsily, running his fingers through his crusty eyelids.

We exchanged glances, staring at each other for what felt like a century.

'Tony?' I said vaguely.

He shook a little.

'Corey?' he replied, practically spelling my name out to me.

He looked nearly the same as he did in our college days, a bit older in the face, but still tall and lanky with that child-like, mischievous grin. But there was something different about his hazel brown eyes, they looked worn, like in the time we were apart he had seen a bit too much of the world for what it was worth.

'Are you and Joanna... you know, together?' I asked, holding out two fingers in which I overlapped.

'Uh, god no!' he exclaimed rather impulsively.

Joanna froze mid-stride between the sliding doors. She gave him a look of death, hanging onto his next sentence.

Tony continued. 'We're just...' he hesitated. 'Seeing

80

each other, you know—we don't wanna put a label on it.'
Tony nodded as if confirming his statement. Joanna must
have shot a look of approval at him because she slipped
out the door to make us coffees without a fuss.

'So, you're fucking,' I said with a smirk.

Caught off guard he nodded, his face turning bright
pink, he hid himself in his t-shirt as he got dressed to
hide his embarrassment. I did the opposite and peeled off
my damp clothes, hanging them on the nearest coat-
hanger. It was like a sauna in there. Joanna had one of
those internal heat pumps and boy did it pump.

Joanna came back with two coffees which she placed
on the glass table before us, careful to not interrupt our
conversation—which took me by surprise. I guess we all
did a lot of growing up since those days that, thank God,
are behind me.

Tony let me wear his t-shirt and a pair of denims. As
I got dressed, I noticed his clothes were carefully folded
into Joanna's drawers, it made me wonder how long he
had been staying with her. Also, there was something
about the way he leaned back into her couch with his feet
resting on the coffee table, taking broad sips from his
mug that said: "NUMBER 1 DAD".

I told him as much as I could about the past five
years of my life broken down to a couple of sentences,
filling in the missing gaps of time which had thrown us
onto opposite ends of the road.

'So,' said Tony, 'the big question is, what next?
You've been robbed of the little you have, you've got no
money, no identification, no passport, how do you expect

to get a job?'

'I haven't thought that far ahead,' I said. 'There's not much else for me to do... I sorta feel stranded in this town, it's a lost cause—shit, *I'm* a lost cause.'

Tony glared at me, refusing to break eye contact. 'I don't have much money left, but I can replace what they took from you.'

'Don't bother,' I said bitterly. 'Maybe my ideas of a cheap escape were never meant to be.'

'Not at all,' he insisted. 'We can make it happen. I know exactly how it feels to be cheated, that's what Accomplished Roofs and Tiles did to me. I was hammering galvanized nails into rooftops sunrise to sunset, working in the extremes of all seasons, yet still, they had the nerve to flick me off like I was a leech on their ankle.' He leaned forward, haunching over his knees, running his hands through his bed-hair while staring into the abyss that came to be his life. 'I walked away with a couple of grand to my name, it didn't take me far, you know, living ain't cheap, especially on this minimum wage shit. Half of my pay went to my landlord, then I'm expected to pull cash outta my ass for groceries. Breaking my back up on those roofs for nothing, man.'

'Sounds like they did you a favour letting you go,' said Joanna, taking a seat next to Tony.

Repulsed by her statement Tony said, 'Favour? I wouldn't go as far to call it that. I'm the one who did them a favour for working for peanuts!' He surveyed the surrounding walls, as if trying to find a way out. 'But that's life, ain't it? Everyone's got a bone to pick with someone over something—shit, even a walk to the shop just to pick up a carton of milk, you'd stumble over someone else's bullshit.'

'Yeah,' said Joanna, 'maybe with your attitude.'

Tony smiled smugly, wrapping his arm around her. 'Like you don't have any problems.'

'I do,' she replied. 'You.'

'Very funny,' he said, fixing his attention back to me. 'Look at you, Cor, you look like a skeleton. The shops down the road open at eight, how bout we get something for that wee thing you call a stomach.'

I perked up. The thought of breakfast lightened the weight on my mind. Primitive necessity, trust it to be the great momentary distraction from internal demise. 'Sounds good, bro,' I said, forcing a smile.

'With what money?' Joanna said. 'You spent your last hundred on the pokies—'

Electrified, Tony pricked up in his seat. 'I was tryna win the jackpot,' he explained. 'I'm not one of those muppets you see at the tavern on a Monday night, I swear. I was thinking big, sometimes that means drastic measures need to be taken.'

'Didn't you receive any compensation from your work?' I asked.

'All I received was a hand-written letter from some faceless douche in management, and a hair from the crack of his ass. Work and Income are taking their sweet ass time delivering my job seeker support as well.' He lit a cigarette, half smiling. 'I guess you could say my life's a bit of a lost cause as well.'

'What about your folks?' I asked. 'They supporting you?'

'They're all I got,' he said, 'but what I got is gone...'

I nodded stonily, wishing I never asked in the first place. 'I bet the shoelaces on my boots everyone in this town feels *down* as the world pretends to be *up*,' I said.

'You can say that again,' said Tony. 'This is about as good as it gets, Cor.' He smiled emphatically, appearing slightly wounded, but this time I understood the source of his infliction.

As the day went on, I soon realized why Tony felt at home at Joanna's. She accommodated our every need. It takes a certain person to go behind their parents back and cater for two unemployed bums with no desire to get a job anytime soon. Tony and I were like that stray dog you found on the streets that your parents wanted no part in. Despite your parents' repulsion, you kept the dog tucked away in the basement—or in Joanna's case, her sleep out—giving it a bed to sleep on and the food scraps your family couldn't eat.

When I thought too hard about the situation it made my stomach uneasy. Nothing but trouble would arise out of this "act of kindness" if you could even call it that. Maybe Joanna was just one lonely girl who needed people to depend on her, and in some twisted way it raised her self-esteem. Whatever her reasons, I put them in the back of my mind along with the other mental clutter I couldn't figure out. Most importantly, Tony was always red-eyed and what I interpreted to be happy, therefore I was happy.

Joanna offered me weed every time she took a hit—which was every ten minutes—I told her weed no longer interested me after the hundredth offer, however, she was nice enough to consider an alternative (Tony let it slip I was a drinker, not a smoker), so she disappeared into her parents' home of all things good and luxurious, returning with a drink to set me straight. I didn't object and joined their 10.A.M party, which probably went on every other day of the week, a cheap remedy to aid the eye clawing dullness of dispersing progress.

***

I shut my eyes and opened them; two weeks had passed me by. My life went from waking up alongside the stench of gutters, to the inviting scent of hot coffee, followed by what Joanna could scavenge from her pantry. Every so often she would bring me a lunch time refreshment, handing me a pint of whiskey. I'd sip on the stuff all afternoon like it was my midday dose of vitamin C. She pinched the booze out of her old man's liquor cabinet. He worked so much he barely had enough time to plough through all the vintage bottles of rum, whiskey, and wine he had accumulated over the years, so I guess you could say I was doing him a favour.

Life couldn't get any sweeter, the only pitfall was passing the two-week threshold with Joanna. Generally, after two weeks spent with anyone, you'll begin to see their shadow-self more than their happy-go-lucky self—and if you're not so lucky, they'll project it onto you.

Joanna didn't necessarily project anything upon me but let's just say I started to notice cracks in her façade, so many, I was led to believe she was yet another broken person.

Through the time distorted ramblings, I found out Joanna received $525 a week from Work and Income for doing absolutely nothing at all. What she earned weekly was what an entry level construction worker would receive for breaking their backs lifting timber and digging holes all day. A regular Work and Income case would receive a minimum of $190 a week, just enough to pay rent and have food for the week if they planned out their meals. Of course, I was eager to discover why she was considered a "privileged case".

As I suspected, she had to jump through many hoops and tick all the right boxes in her medical report. She claimed she had agoraphobia and made a point to the doctor he couldn't refuse: *If I can't walk past my letter box, what makes you think I can go to work?* The doctor gave her case worker the thumbs-up as well as a hefty prescription of drugs she didn't know how to pronounce. In spite of this, she sold them off to eager addicts and wasters of life alike.

She joked about how she played the *professionals* with the agoraphobic card, but really, if you kept your eyes on her—and not in a pipe piece—you'd be able to see what I saw. For starters, Joanna always got her drugs delivered, if for some reason her prescription—or weed—couldn't be delivered and needed to be picked up, she would cry and throw a tantrum to her mother until she bowed down to her will. Sickening, right? But the real question is, what part? The fact her mother drops by to a drug dealers house on her daughters accord, the same way she would at the grocery store to pick up a loaf of bread, handing it over discreetly saying, "Don't tell your father." I guess the apple doesn't fall too far from the tree. Her mother was a secret stoner, kept it from her husband for nearly twenty years, but that's another story completely. So really, I didn't blame Joanna for her deceptive ways, no behaviour goes on without being taught.

But anyway, I know my previous statement sounds vague, but believe me, the tiniest details reveal someone's true nature. Another example that suggested Joanna was actually agoraphobic was how she paid the neighbour's kid to walk her dog, just to keep her parents off her back. But the avoidance gets more extreme. She does everything for Tony on the inside, whereas Tony does everything for her on the out, this is when her mum builds up the courage to say no. It's like a manic episode Tony got tangled up in, manifesting itself as some twisted compromise.

Maybe I'm over thinking all of this and in reality, she's just beyond the word lazy, but anyway, I've broken down the façade she's built, and it dawned on me every aspect of her life is governed by avoidance. Don't get any wrong ideas, I know it sounds like I'm being harsh and hating on her, I'm really not, it just pisses me off how people construct these intricate masks to make themselves feel better about their flaws, rather than facing it head on, and actually making a change for the betterment of not only themselves, but the people who surround them. Most of these anomalies I'm talking about are a subconscious reflex, a strategy the ego uses to defend itself from its sworn enemy; truth. But maybe I just have too much time on my hands, and my brain's just ticking like the clock on the wall, after all, a person who works against time, has *time* to think, not act.

Chapter 8

A trip down memory lane.

A lane I walk every day.

I can still see your face, but you fade a little more through each reflection.

Will I ever see you again?

Or is it only through death can I see you clearly? For here I only see darkly.

Who really knows when death will be knocking on your door anyway?

When I was younger, I liked the idea of dying for a purpose, but I didn't quite foresee how these chains of events would bring me so much closer to death. Maybe it was a part of the plan and, as humans, we are only supposed to know so much in order to fulfil our destinies. Maybe if we did know we would screw up the greater plan entirely before we even took that very first step into the wonder filled suburbs of our hometown. But the wonder would quickly turn on us the farther we walk, until it's too late and there's no turning back. Then we are lost, left to our own devices, caught in the gloom of what we were led to believe was paradise.

As creative creatures of the earth we are granted the power of choice, we succeed, we fail, we thrive, or wither away. In my case, I slowly burnt out like a dimly lit candle, blown out by those who breathed their vengeance upon me. As for some, they allowed their flame to burn out, neglecting the sustenance their souls required to blossom as they turn to stone on suburban stoops, rinsing and drying, placing them self onto a shelf, becoming a tacky ornament people use to praise for its ability to light up the room. Now, they're forgotten—some dismissed for their ugly bitterness—and begin to collect dust on the mantel piece, not even being rinsed or left out to dry to be reused but left to themselves to die.

Some dowse their flame in water, bringing it all to an end in one quick silent explosion within the self, and just like that, their flame vanishes, never to be seen again. Sounds simple, doesn't it? But going out this way will only send a ripple of shattering dismay into the once wholesome hearts of those threaded to the deceased.

A crack in the heart forms—for the less fortunate a hole, a hole which can never be repaired, no matter how many ailments are administered.

But some of us are born with a hole in our heart. Alone, we struggle to maintain the strength of a soldier as we step out into the big, wide world to fight another day in our own private war. I knew I'd stumble across many broken hearts in my time, but not at the age of thirteen.

It was first period at Saint Aberdeen college, Mr. Boyce pranced around the white board, praising the students who actively participated. It wasn't hard to spot the high achievers by the way their stiff backs rose high to meet the white board. Mr. Boyce looked like a dried-up prune who was older than the textbooks before us, textbooks that remained closed on mine and Tony's desks.

Tony and I leaned back in our chairs in the back row, goofing about, doing what we did any other day of the week in religious education class. Seated behind his desk, Tony towered over the rest of us third formers who were yet to endure puberty. He stood out amongst the rest, whether it was his hair that was on fire, or his mouthful of cheek, and compassionate hazel brown eyes which reassured you it was okay to be yourself.

In between our laughter, I decided to break my eraser apart into tiny pieces and throw them at the students in the front row. They twitched when the shards of eraser struck their ears. However, they refused to withdraw their focus and keenly listened to Mr. Boyce's endless drool about the sins of man, as if his words came straight out of the saint's mouth.

On Tony's desk, resting beside his notebook he was scribbling cartoons into, was a novel with a photograph he used as a bookmarker. Out of curiosity I snatched the book off his desk and opened it to the marked page. With wild flapping hands Tony attempted to snatch back his book. I shielded his hands by turning my back on him and pulled out the photograph. It was a black and white picture of a young ginger haired girl dressed in a skirt flaring out at the ends. Tony gave up trying to retrieve the photo and sunk down in his chair. He craned his neck over my shoulder and tried to read my thoughts.

'Is this your girlfriend?' I asked mockingly, turning back to him with the picture held out.

Tony reached out and plucked the picture out of my hands and used his blue sweater to wipe away any fingerprints.

'It's my mum,' he said, staring into the photo glowingly.

I broke into fits of laughter. 'Why do you have a picture of your mum?'

'Because she's dead,' he said contently.

This startled me. Not only the way he announced it so calmly, but the fact I had been so ignorant. The smirk on my face faded. 'Oh, shit… I'm… I'm sorry, man,' I said.

'It's okay,' said Tony, patting me on the back. 'You didn't know.'

'When did she die?' I asked.

His eyes were still fixed to the photograph. 'A long time ago. I was just a boy,' he said vaguely.

Tony slipped the picture back into the book and tucked it into the security of his backpack. Based upon his response, I decided not to impose and changed the subject. It was then my little thirteen-year-old brain realized Tony had more than a few cracks in his heart compared to the other school kids. The one who had given him life had gone up and disappeared, kept alive only by his precious memories.

From this day onward I saw Tony through different eyes. Who would have known? Tony was the funniest guy I knew at school. He was quirky, weird, and didn't care what the other kids thought about him, or whether or not they understood him. He was himself, and happy to be himself, unlike most kids our age.

I went on with throwing bits of eraser at the students in the front row, but this time I went by noticed. Mr. Boyce's bug eyes bulged from out of his wrinkly eye sockets, he raised a finger, pointing it at me with searing conviction. The murmurs from the other students fell silent. All eyes were on me. Immediately, I regretted disrupting his class.

'You!' Boyce exclaimed.

I turned pink, lowering my head to my empty desktop.

'*Get down on your knees and beg for my forgiveness! God is ashamed of you; Jesus is ashamed of you... Your mother is ashamed of you! Get out of my classroom!*'

The moment I was exiled from Boyce's class was the moment that tipped me over the edge. I had been hovering over the edge for some time now. All I needed was one little push, and the fallen angels would rise from out of the pools of darkness, waiting to catch me as I fell.

Chapter 9

Complacency is the silent killer of anything extraordinary, and all things extraordinary will inevitably lead us to our death. When broken down, life is really a one-way street, the only difference being, some spend their lives stacking blocks in the direction of the sky. The height of the stack signifies what you've accomplished and how far you've stretched out your wings. Whereas others, such as myself, fell through the cracks of the building blocks of life, reaching out to anyone who would pull us out from our rut, in hope of guiding us to a better day.

I remember hearing Homeless Harry once say, 'No tree grows to the sky.' Meaning, it's only a matter of time before our tree withers at its roots, or worse, is chopped down by the hands of others. If only I knew those helping hands that reached out to me would eventually turn on me. If I had acquired this knowledge earlier, I would have gone about this situation differently, but there's nothing I can do now except for reflect on my wrong doings.

I can't help but think maybe I could have saved a life, or two. Then again, the coming of wisdom is never on time, mistakes always arrive first.

It all started one Wednesday morning when Tony said something like, 'Here's some cash Joanna gave me, could you go to the shop and get me some smokes?'

'You got two legs, don't you?' I replied.

He sighed and said, 'I'm in one of those cagey moods. I can't think about anything worse than people knowing I exist right now. I'd rather be like, say, the wind.'

'The wind?'

'You know, its present but you can't see it, get my gist?'

'Yeah, yeah,' I muttered. 'It's too early in the morning to be all metaphoric.'

He clambered about under the bed and pulled out some crusty denims, giving them a sniff before shrugging and putting them on anyway.

'Off ya hop,' he said. 'This is the only time of day I get to myself.'

Grinning, I said, 'Don't do anything I wouldn't do.'

He laughed. 'The thing is, Cor, what haven't you done? You're just as saintly as Joanna's knickers.' He flicked her G-string at me, which I deflected in the last second.

'On that note, I'm out,' I said turning for the door.

'Yeah, get outta here. Don't be in no rush would ya!'

The sliding door clicked shut behind me. I zipped my

coat up, crossed through the backyard, and headed for the driveway. At this hour, Joanna's parents were at work. We were free to roam as we pleased. At least that's what I thought.

The heart-stopping sound of the back door slamming shut meant only two things. One, Joanna had a quick shower, highly unlikely, two, her parents were home.

An ape of a man hurled a big black rubbish bag over one shoulder and proceeded to dump it in the bin. My feet turned to ice. He slowly arched his head over his shoulder, his eyes widening as my presence became apparent. He had the same bushy black eyebrows as Joanna. His stomach was round, but his shoulders were broad and deadly. He was dressed in a collared shirt, with a loose tie around his neck.

'What the bloody fuck do think you're doing on my property?'

The back door popped open. Joanna appeared in her dressing gown with a towel wrapped around her head, holding a tray with three cups of coffee, and three plates with marmite on toast.

Her father gawked at the tray. 'You!' he barked, hardly sounding human at all.

He ran right for me. It was a savage kind of run. He wanted blood. He wanted me hammered and tenderized before he devoured me. I retreated to the sleep-out, yanking on the door with all my might. It was locked. The curtains were drawn shut. I hammered my fist into the glass, screaming and shouting for Tony's help.

Tony emerged. Looking all sweaty and flustered. He

was butt naked with a porno magazine covering his cock.

'Open the fucking door!' I shouted.

It was too late. I had been snapped. Mr. Stevenson grabbed me by the hood on my jacket and pulled me into a headlock. In the background Joanna screamed and pleaded. 'Dad! Leave him alone! Please, don't hurt him!'

'I'll do more than fucking hurt him, honey!' Mr. Stevenson grunted, grinding my neck into his armpit.

Tony stood in the doorway with a look of sheer terror on his face. Out of shock, he dropped his porno magazine to the floor, giving us a million-mile stare. Mr. Stevenson jerked his head up and peered at Tony through the glass. He went pale, his jaw dropping. Mr. Stevenson then released me as he stared blankly at Tony's erection. This lapse in attention gave Tony enough time to unlock the door and pull me inside. But Mr. Stevenson flipped out again, as if Tony's erect penis made him that much more angry. 'I'll break this fucking door open with my fist, if you don't come out now!' he kept saying. He shielded his eyes with his hands and peered through the glass. His eyes on the empty bottles of vintage scotch whiskey I stacked on the dresser. There must have been at least ten of them. He exploded from the inside out. 'You fucking little shits! Those bottles are worth more than your lives! I'll kill you! Fuckin' slit your throat!' He made a slicing gesture around his neck. Tony pulled the curtain and threw whatever he could in front of the door.

Then there was silence. Even Joanna had stopped wailing in the background. We glanced at each other. Both of us panting heavily, unsure of what to do next.

Tony sighed and rested his back on the wall. Above him a little window was open by a few inches. Suddenly, hairy hands seeped through the little window and scooped up Tony's scrawny body and began to choke the life out of him. To start with, I thought all of this was a plain and simple form of fatherly rage. I was wrong.

If I attempted to free Tony maybe Joanna's dad would grab me with the other hand, and choke us both to death, I thought. Too many thoughts flowed through my mind, so many I acted on impulse. I grabbed an empty bottle of scotch, smashed it on the dresser, and poked the jagged handle into Mr. Stevenson's forearm.

He yelped and released his hold on Tony. Then he went hysterical and ripped his shirt off, wrapping it around his wound. With no outlet for his aggression, he went right for Joanna. We watched on helplessly as he threw a savage right fist straight into her gut. She fell to the grass, too winded to shriek in pain. 'This is your fault!' he shouted. 'You're full of secrets! Just like your mother!' He kicked her in the ribs with his pointy ended leather shoes too many times to count, until she appeared to lose consciousness.

'We gotta do something,' I said to Tony, who was shocked into submission.

He snapped out of his trance and started throwing on whatever clothes were nearby. 'We gotta run! Take off to the fucking hills for all I care!'

There was an ear wrenching crack on the glass door, followed by a shattering secondary blow. Mr. Stevenson took to his tool shed and fetched his sledgehammer while we were running around like rats in a cage.

'The little window,' Tony said quickly. 'Out—now.'

I rocked back the hinges as far as they would go and pulled myself through. Tony did the same. Joanna's dad ploughed through the glass just as Tony slipped out. We bypassed our regular point of entry (the wonky timber fence) and leaped over it instead, making a break into the openness of the field.

***

Rain trickled down our faces as we cut across the rugby field to the town centre. The showers quickly turned into dismal rain. We regrouped outside the Four Square, catching our breath as we sat on the sidewalk, looking like teenage misfits who had nothing better to do other than hurl abuse at locals for entertainment.

'We can't stay here,' I said. 'Did you see the state of Joanna's dad? In no time he'll zip around the corner, hunting us down.'

Tony laughed at this. 'He looked like a kettle about to boil over,' he said, flicking his cigarette into the gutter.

'We need to find shelter—somewhere less exposed.' I said, keeping my eyes peeled for cars driving at crazy speeds.

'I know a place,' said Tony. 'It's a bit of a walk, but nothing you can't handle.' He pointed west to a daunting peak shrouded in fog. 'There's a trail leading up to the foothills, takes you to Brown Owl if you go all the way. On the way up there's a cabin with a fireplace. Could be a place to rest up for the night.'

'Anywhere is better than here,' I said, stepping to my feet.

After thirty minutes of walking, we passed a paddock with two horses all rugged up in wet weather gear. On the way over we didn't take any chances and jumped in nearby hedges whenever a car raced past us. In no time we were pushed into no-man's land, scaling along the edges of the civilized world. Nothing but forested pine hills and inhospitable peaks greeted us as we trudged through the long-wet grass, following a boggy dirt path up hill.

'This place is known to the locals as Magic Mountain,' Tony said. 'Shrooms use to grow everywhere round here. They had so much to offer the people, but people took, and took—the way they do—now, nothing.'

I was too shaken to have a conversation. Tony didn't seem to care. I shifted my focus to my wet socks to ease my anxiety. We climbed an incline that refused to cease, the trail became a murky creek spewing brown water downhill. We trampled over loose rocks, losing our footing more than once, our knees straining through every step until, finally, we arrived at the cabin.

Tony ran to the edge of the ridge, I trailed behind. 'If you look out there,' he pointed, 'we have Kapati coast.' He retraced his steps back to where the trail declined. 'And on the opposite peak—you can't see it cos it's too foggy—you have Manaaki Falls. The trail leads all the way out to the coast of Eastbourne.' He smiled to himself. 'When I was little my mum used to take me up there, of course, I never made it to the top, but she used to tell me 'bout it.'

'It's a shame we can't see it. Come on,' I said, putting a hand on his shoulder, 'let's get to the cabin.'

Tony fiddled with the doorknob. 'It's locked. Probably only open during summer.' He peered up at the gruesome sky. 'If summer will ever come again.'

'What're we gonna do?' I asked. 'We can't stay out here.'

Tony shrugged. Then he took two steps back and charged through the door. It burst open with a painful groan. He grinned at me and said, 'If anyone asks, we were desperate hikers who needed shelter.' We went straight for the fireplace and got to work. Within a bucket there were strips of kindling as well as newspapers and a box of matches. Chopped blocks of pine were stacked in a neat pile against the wall. 'Leave it to me,' said Tony. 'Believe it or not, I was a cadet once upon a time.' In less than ten minutes he had the fire roaring and the little cabin started to heat up like an oven.

I stripped down to my jocks and hung my wet clothes on the line in front of the fire. Tony did the same. 'Heat rises,' he said. 'Once we turn this place into a sauna, bunk up top.' He climbed a wooden ladder with peeling blue paint, hunkering down in the bunk closest to the fireplace. He curled up on the thin foam mattress and started to read a novel he found in the bucket filled with kindling. Half of the pages were ripped out; some desperate hiker must have used it to start a fire.

I turned the cabin upside down, searching for

anything I considered to be of use. I found three tins of tuna along with half a packet of stale crackers. It wasn't much, but it was food to see us through until tomorrow. I stoked the fire and couldn't stop thinking about how pissed Mr. Stevenson was. I wondered if Joanna was okay, unable to erase the memories of Mr Stevenson stomping on his own daughter's ribs.

Come dinner time we sat on the floor and ate in silence, reaching a drought in conversation. No humour slid off our tongues. There was nothing to be chirpy about. No achievements. No destination. No plan. Just two miserable twenty-year-old's, sitting side by side in their undies, eating tuna out of tins with their hands, staring frightfully into the fire as we realized this is the type of people we have become.

It became clear to me we were officially off the grid. We were social misfits banished to the pine riddled hilltops, left to dwindle in solitude. There was no place for us in the civilized world. It all made so much sense. Getting the boot out of town within itself marked us both as outcasts, unfit for the civilized world. Together, we had failed the systems trials and tests, we defied our mentors and spat in the face of our noble teachers. Disgraced them. Erased them. Now look at us.

I found some candles in a drawer full of cobwebs and sparked a match, lighting all four of them, placing them in each corner of the cabin. The overcast skies and the absence of moonlight made me feel like we had been swallowed by the forces of darkness. The faint glow at the end of Tony's cigarette, which puckered to the side of his mouth, seemed to be our only defence against this all-encompassing gloom. The same void filled silence we shared over dinner followed us outside where we smoked beneath the veranda.

'I don't know what I'm doing with my life,' Tony said soberly. Through the glowing ember of his cigarette, I could see his eyes were tense. Serious emotion surged behind his eyes. I knew he wanted to breakdown there and then, shed a tear and have a moment. But he wouldn't. He wasn't brought up to be like that. 'I don't know where to go,' he said absently, staring out into the void. 'I'm down to my last twenty, soon I'll have no money, no food, no shelter—'

'We've got the cabin for now,' I broke in, hoping to ease his worries.

'Fuck the cabin,' he snapped. 'You and I both know this is no place we can call home.'

'We have to stay present in the moment,' I said. 'We sure as hell can't make any *real* changes with our worries. When I was down and out in Wellington city, Homeless Harry taught me that. Only in the *now* can we shape our realities. When you're on the street, it's all you've got, that is if you wanna survive. The past will only slow you down and worrying about the future will make you hesitate when your moment comes to strike.'

Tony handed me his cigarette. I took a couple of drags and then passed it back to him.

'Well,' he began, 'that Homeless Harry sounds like a wise man. On the bright side, if there is one, maybe all of this was a good thing—you know, for the betterment of our soul's development, like that shit you always go on about once you've had a few too many drinks.'

'What was?'

'Getting kicked out of Joanna's. I couldn't keep stringing her along like this anyway, just so my selfish needs got met, that's not the kinda guy I am.' Tony gazed into the abyss once again. 'But that's the kind of person I'm becoming… and that's what I'm afraid of, Corey. I'm losing myself, I'm afraid I'll never find the person I use to be.'

'You know what I'm sick of?' I said, snatching the smoke out of his mouth, puffing on it greedily. 'Moving round from town to town—yeah, transience has its moments, but an equal amount of pitfalls. I just want peace. A quiet space. But you know what?'

'What?' Tony asked, hanging onto my words.

'I'll never find peace here. Not in this town. Not in this country, and certainly not in this world. To exist is to suffer, and for what? Shit, I don't know—no one knows, people pretend to know, but when their time finally comes to leave this place, they choke-up and second guess all those cheap ideas they recited to themselves to keep them going.'

'So what you're saying is your final solution is knocking on deaths door, huh?' Tony asked with a smirk.

'It's the only door that leads us outta here.'

'Well then, guess what? The only way back is south.'

Chapter 10

Overnight the skies cleared. Asides from the pine covered hills congested in morning fog, it was a crisp, blue winters day. One of those days where the mere sight of a clean blue sky grants you the confidence to begin again, but not for Tony. Tony wasn't as enthusiastic as I was about the clean-slate the canvas-like sky painted for us. He was still held within the clutches of last nights' funk.

He threw the last of his money at me, twenty dollars in coins, burying himself underneath his jacket in attempt to block out the sun and anything representing beginnings. I collected the coins and stuffed them in my pockets. I understood his anguish, I too resonated with his sense of displacement. But I knew we had to keep moving forward. If we stayed here nothing new would come our way, I knew from somewhere deep within, Tony knew this, also. Like what Homeless Harry use to say to me, "the only way to change your life is to interact with it, get to know it, befriend it."

Back in town smoke rose from brick-laid chimneys, I inhaled the smoky pine, releasing a satisfied sigh, thinking, *ah, the smell of winter*. To my right there were two enormous peaks cloaked in fog. I guessed the cabin was located somewhere below the summit. From here it looked like the peaks had been harnessing all the ugliness of the world and pouring it over us, just to make our lives that much more unclear, yet there was beauty present—at least from afar, cold, bitter beauty.

Up ahead the town square came into sight. There was a hairdressers, a fish and chip shop, and the Four-Square mini mart. All of them were closed except for the Four Square—everything was always closed in this sleepy town.

The Four Square reeked of cigarette smoke infused with incense. I figured the clerk often burnt it to disguise the fact he nipped out back for a couple of sneaky puffs as he waited for the handful of customers he received each day.

I greeted him as I grabbed a shopping basket and made my way down one of only two aisles. The Indian clerk greeted me in the same way he would to someone entering his shop with a hockey-mask. I felt his eyes stabbing into my back, conscious of my every move, every tremor from my eyelid.

The motion detector at the shop entrance buzzed again. A guy with his hair clipped down to a shadow waltzed in, giving the clerk a hollow nod of the head. He appeared to be around my age but the way he carried himself suggested he was much older. He was dressed in a black hoodie with a leather jacket pulled over the top, dark jeans and steel capped boots, tattoos swirled around his neck. He was clean cut, yet there was nothing clean about him. He eyeballed me for a while as if he wanted me to know he knew my face and wouldn't forget it.

I watched him. Bemused by his loud energy which filled up the store like a stereo playing at full volume. He stopped in his tracks, gliding his hand along his scalp. Then he frantically patted his leather jacket down as if he had forgotten something. Relieved, he pulled out a black beanie from his pocket and covered up his bald head.

He approached the counter and instead of purchasing an item, the clerk bought something off him. I picked up a box of cereal and pretended to read the back, occasionally glancing up at the exchange when I felt it was safe. The clerk handed him a bundle of bills in a not-so-discreet handshake, meanwhile, the guy dropped what I interpreted to be a tiny baggie of some sort on the floor, then he strolled out of the shop like he was off to church.

I dropped the box of cereal into my basket, trying to look a tad more casual than their exchange, and moved up the aisle, getting closer to the counter to get a better look.

The shop keeper came out with a broom and swept in the direction where the baggie was dropped. As he was doing this, he caught my eyes and unknowingly started sweeping at his feet. Simultaneously our eyes dropped to the baggie, then returned to one another.

'What's this!' he exclaimed. 'Bloody kids bringing drugs into my shop.' He proceeded to pick up the baggie and slipped it into his trouser pocket. 'I'm calling the police,' he said, disappearing out back.

Not too long after he returned to the counter and I paid for the items. 'Forgetting something?' I said, gesturing to his phone that he left on the counter.

His eyes widened. He snatched the phone and dialled 111 without linking the call. Pressing his phone to his ear he said unconvincingly, 'This used to be a good place to live a couple of years ago.'

'And you're sure doing a damn good job keeping the town safe,' I said, taking my change.

I exited the shop with the shopping in one hand and my change in the other. I was too immersed in trying to slip every cent into my pocket, I was oblivious to the silver SUV whose one and only desire was to flatten me on the pavement. The lunatic behind the wheel put his foot down and charged toward me. I dodged the front bumper with less than a second to spare. Although, one of the headlights clipped my shopping bag, sending all the slices of bread flying.

I recognized the savage behind the wheel. What other maniac wished to run me down? I could think of a couple of people, but none of them came close to how pissed off Mr. Stevenson looked.

I nodded to myself in silent defeat. Eventually, you've got to lose a few before you start winning. Plus, he kinda had me cornered outside the hairdressers.

'You muthafuckin' cunt!' he blurted. He slammed the

driver's door shut, grumbling incomprehensibly. I saw what looked like a fully loaded 22 resting in between the cup holder in the front seat. Tony wasn't joking when he brought up the idea of Mr. Stevenson hunting us down with a rifle the night before. I don't know what scared me more; the fact Mr. Stevenson chose to bring a loaded gun, or how Tony voiced the rifles involvement with humour and calm knowings.

However pissed, he left the 22 to rest, and instead lugged a barbarian sized piece of wood from the trunk.

'I want you outta Totra Park—fuck, I want you gone off the face of the piecea shit earth!'

'Mr,' I said rationally and slowly, careful to keep my voice contained and non-threatening. 'Put down the bit of wood. Me and Tony are dead to you and your family, I swear. You won't ever see our faces again.'

'Think again if I'm gonna let you off that easy! Both you degenerates screwing my daughter at the same time, like some perverted Sunday spit roast, drinking all my scotch that's—'

'—Worth more than me and Tonys' lives combined, I know...'

'It's worth more than your goddamn souls served on a platter,' he snarled, raising the piece of timber above his head.

'Now, now, that's no way to speak to a member of the community,' said the same punk from the store. He removed his leather jacket and hoodie throwing it into the backseat of his rust-bucket car—maybe in the eighties it would have been a shimmering turd-brown

Commodore—now it looked like something someone had picked up from a junkyard.

The punk fearlessly strolled over to Mr. Stevenson and I. His mere presence seemed to deflate Mr. Stevenson's ego; my stomach even felt a little uneasy within his presence. He had anarchy tattoos on either side of his muscular arms. One tattoo in particular stood out to me, it was of a skeleton with its tongue poked out, on its tongue was a tab of LSD, the anarchy symbol decorated the blotter.

'You better put that thing away before I'm forced to preform citizen's arrest,' he said, lifting his white singlet up, revealing a 9mm tucked into his underpants.

Mr. Stevenson's hands began to tremble so violently, the bit of timber in his hands danced like a flag caught in the wind.

'This isn't over,' he stammered, red faced and flustered. 'Not until I have both you and your mates balls pinned to the wall beside my bowling trophies!'

'So, are we cool now, Mr. Stevenson?' I asked.

'The Nazis thought Poland was cool before they decided to fuck them, course we're not fuckin' cool, you good for nothing bludger!'

Keeping the punk in the corner of his eye, he jumped into his SUV and raced off.

'You okay?' he asked.

I nodded. 'We better get outta here before we're plagued by the cops.'

'Don't sweat it,' he said, glancing at the Four-Square. 'There's nothing to worry about.'

Then I remembered his exchange with the clerk. My mind stopped spinning.

'About that,' I began, 'thanks for your help, me and my mate had a—'

'Save your story, we've all got one,' he cut in. 'Most important thing is you won't be tied up in the back of some specy old cunts boot.'

We talked for a bit longer, enough for me to learn his name was Todd.

'Where you from?' he asked. 'Hop in, I'll give you a lift.'

I hesitated. Not knowing how to articulate mine and Tony's situation. 'I live *over there*.' I made thundering gestures over the western hill tops.

Todd nodded slowly, not breaking eye contact. 'Well, do you wanna ride *over there* or what?'

What good would it do hiding from the truth, I thought. Of all people this guy looked like he might understand. 'Me and my mate are living in the bush, got nowhere to go, nowhere to be.'

'No shit?' he replied, starting up the car. 'I'll take you to the trail head.'

We drove down Tucker Street, a long and narrowing residential area with cottages nestled on either side of the road. Todd steered the car with his knees as he rolled a smoke. Once he finished, he passed his rolling tobacco to me and said, 'Roll some up for you and your buddy. What did you say your mates' name was?'

'I didn't. His name's Tony. Tony McKnight.' Tony was quite popular in town, so I thought I'd add in his last name, just in case Todd had heard of him.

'Tony McKnight!' he exclaimed, bashing the steering wheel. 'I know that lanky ranga! Gets around town, doesn't he?'

'Just consult your local GP, he'll tell you all about him,' I said laughing, feeling a hint of happiness which almost felt foreign.

The road thinned out as well as the residential area. In less than a glance we were on our way out of town. In place of the homes were sheep in paddocks enclosed in a dreary haze. Todd pulled into the trail head car park. The same horses came into sight to the left of the trail, still rugged up in their wet weather gear. For some reason Tony was in the car park standing on the other side of the fence, feeding the horses bundles of fresh grass. Cabin fever must've gotten the best of him.

Todd skidded over the gravel and swung into a parking bay. 'Tony!' he yelled with a demented grin on his face. He hopped out of the car and staggered over the long, wet grass. 'So, it's true,' he said. 'Here I was thinking your buddy was having me on!' They shook hands and pulled each other in for a half-hug. 'How long has it been? Haven't seen you since Kieran's party.'

'Yeah,' Tony replied glumly.

'What's your deal? Your mates been telling me you've been playing fucked up family with Joanna Stevenson. Mate, what were you thinking… were you even?'

Tony's face went redder than his hair. 'I didn't have too much of a choice,' he said.

After a shallow conversation with Todd, it didn't take

long to realize he was a rebel without a cause. A small fish in an even smaller bowl. But every rebel had a cause—or at least someone to blame for their actions—even if that cause was just as messed up as eating with the same spoon his mum used to cook smack on when he was a kid. But as I'd later learn, there was a lot more to Todd than his tough-guy persona.

Tony told Todd about how he had been laid off from work—he told anyone who'd listen to him rant on about corporate conspiracy (as he labelled it) and how we were all unconsciously pawns on their giant earthly chessboard. If you let him harp on for more than five minutes, he'd tell you about how he reckoned corporations were so rich, they bought a thing called contemporary consciousness—which we contemplate, but ultimately adhere to—and sold it to us until we, ourselves, settled on their idea and called it existence.

Todd took great interest in Tony's spiel, maybe it served as a valid excuse to justify his disobedience toward the law. I could tell by the way he lifted an eyebrow, half smiling, his eyes twitching ever so slightly, it could easily go by unnoticed, like the way someone's eyes dart around words inside a book. But whatever he was thinking he kept it to himself, giving Tony as much room to speak. For a moment, a second no more, I could have sworn I saw cash symbols flashing within his eyes, the way the big billboards shine on endless Wellington city nights. Then Todd's eyes switched back to this charming, empathetic glimmer, until Tony burnt himself out.

'Sounds like they got you good,' said Todd, offering a

smoke to each of us. 'Say, Tony, how you feel about helping me out, and at the same time, I know some people who can dish you out some redemption, what's it they say? Scratch my back, I'll scratch yours.'

Tony glanced at me, hoping to catch a glimpse of my approval. After all, we were in this together. I didn't steer him into any potholes of my opinions and took a mutual stance, wanting to see where Todd was going with this.

'Go ahead,' said Tony. The moment those two words left his mouth, a door to a new world creaked open. But who'd have thought later down the track I'd be the one who led us all the way in.

'You mentioned how you and the boys at Accomplished were roofing beside the Trentham racecourse? Correct me if I'm wrong, but isn't the construction site alongside a retirement village?'

'Yeah,' Tony murmured, 'what's it to you?'

'What're we talking about here in terms of inventory? Padlocked shipping containers? Or is the crew driving in and out with all their utilities?'

'They store all their tools in shipping containers— why you ask?' Tony replied, a little too rapidly.

'Perfect,' Todd muttered, stubbing out his smoke with the end of his boot.

'What exactly are you gonna do?' asked Tony. 'I don't want any trouble—'

'Relax. I don't want to leave any scars on anyone— unless you want me to,' he added while grinning. 'It's not what I'm gonna do that should worry you, but what *you're* gonna do… that is, if you wanna make some money.' He

114

peered over at me. 'The offer goes for you, too. We could use someone on our team who's the silent type, most of them don't know how to keep their mouth shut.'

'We're not interested,' I said.

'Ah, he has a voice,' said Todd. 'For a second I thought someone had cut out your tongue.' He laughed to himself. 'Sorta like this chick I used to know—and from what I've heard, Tony knows quite well also.'

Tony's ears pricked up.

'Well,' Todd continued, 'her tongue wasn't exactly cut out, but she's got half of one. But you'd know all about that, wouldn't you, Tony?'

'Tess,' Tony murmured. 'You know Tessa?'

Todd smirked and nodded slowly. 'Believe me, the whole town knows Tess, just like they know you. So, you boys wanna make some fast, easy money?'

Tony thought about it for a second. He was already down and out, holding no more than a couple of cents to his name. My funds were even bleaker. 'We're in,' he said.

'Dude, just think about what you're getting yourself in to,' I said. 'This will attract nothing but trouble.'

Tony pulled me aside, putting his arm over my shoulder and steered me in the direction of his desires. 'If you do this with me, I'll buy you the best gear for your northern adventure, no strings attached.'

'Who do you think I am?' I said, pulling away from his hold on me. 'I've had nothing for the past five years, what makes you think I give a shit about a pile of overpriced gear?'

'Just come along for the ride. I can't do *this* by

myself.'

'Then don't do it,' I said. 'I'm not interested.'

'Oh, come on,' said Todd, 'You can't leave your buddy hanging.' Todd retreated to his vehicle. 'I'll leave the two of you alone to figure out what you wanna do. In the meantime, enjoy mother nature. I hear she's scheduled for another storm tonight; hope you've got enough wood in your cabin.' He smirked, revved the engine, and skidded over the gravel, dropping his handbrake as he drifted around the bend.

I did hang onto Todd's words well after he left, but it was Tony who roped me in. But then again, I did leave him hanging.

***

A few days later at sunset we waited for Todd outside the spear tipped gates of the racecourse. *We*, as in Tony dragged me along with him. I didn't really have much of a choice, as Tony put it, 'We'd only be feeling sorry for ourselves at the cabin."

Todd was in the passenger seat of a black Ute. In the driver's seat was a guy called Jay who looked like he was recently released from prison. I had no idea what we were in for, neither did Tony, but it didn't stop us from blindly accepting Todd's offer, which promised no more than trespassing on private property and possibly committing arson. Before we squeezed into the back of the Ute, Todd threw high visibility vests at us and told us to put them on.

'Get in the goddamn car,' Jay grunted, craning his neck around in all directions. Probably keeping an eye out for cops. We cruised down a brand-new tar-sealed road with the train tracks heading north to our left, and the retirement village to our right—yellow brick houses spanning east as far as the eyes could see. Asides from the odd granny driving by at a snail's pace, it was quieter than the deathly silence that loomed among the resident's homes.

A padlocked gate came into sight, blocking off our chances of moving into the construction site. Attached to the gate were various signs stating: *Safety vest required. Now entering hazardous site.*

'Fuck!' Todd grumbled, bashing the dashboard. 'You didn't say anything about a locked gate!'

'I didn't know,' Tony explained. 'Me and the boys use to knock off at four-thirty, the site manager was the last to leave and probably locked up around five-thirty.'

'Half an hour ago,' said Todd, checking the time on the dash.

'He'll be well on his way to Kapati by now,' Tony added.

'What's the big deal?' I said. 'You've got bolt cutters in the tray. It's not like we're gonna leave this place unnoticed, we may as well let ourselves in.'

'Yeah,' Todd agreed. 'Good thinking—was it, Corey?'

I smiled and nodded.

Todd tilted his head in the direction of the gate, his brain ticking. He raised his hand in face of the construction site like a Greek warrior commanding a chariot and shouted, 'Jay, full speed!'

Jay unflinchingly put his foot down and drove right through the flimsy gate. Further up the road, there were a handful of portable site facilities scattered over the rich, brown soil speckled in gravel and other jagged pieces of steel. Timber frames were mounted upon slabs of concrete as if they were the bones of houses to be. Various shipping containers rested side by side on the last remaining patches of decaying grass, soon to be demolished by diggers come Monday. Jay steered the Ute off-road. We rocked from side to side over the uneven mounds of dirt, dodging the knife-blade roofing tiles. Jay put the Ute into low gear and weaved around the offcuts.

'What shipping container is it?' Todd asked Tony.

'The white one.'

'What are you clowns waiting for!' he said. 'The bolt cutters are in the tray, me and Jay will keep watch.'

Tony snatched the bolt cutters like he was a part-time criminal and clipped the padlock open. He pried open the clunky steel doors as they moaned in rusted discomfort. All that was in the container was a heap of rusted tools not even I'd want to use.

'Don't look so disappointed,' Tony said. 'It might not look like much, but this stuff is worth a fortune—especially all the tiles.'

He wheeled out the guillotine, meanwhile Jay backed the Ute as close as he could get to the container. 'Clear it out!' Todd called out. 'We don't have much time. Tony, pick and choose what you think will be of the most value.'

Together, we hurled out boxes of galvanized nails as Jay strapped the guillotine onto the tray. With all the goods loaded, we drove into the blanketing dusk. I glanced out the window as the sun and moon caught my eye, hanging in the sky at a perfect fifty-fifty contrast like the Yin and Yang. But where we were headed, the darkness outlived the light.

Chapter 11

Two long days of staring at the cabin walls passed us by. We filled the emptiness of our day by smoking and mindless talk about what we'd do with our money once Todd pulled through. Eventually Tony received a call from Todd explaining how the tools were auctioned off to a local business whose name will remain anonymous.

We anxiously awaited our pay check. We didn't expect too much, but a cut of the deal went without saying. But not a cent came our way. Once again, we had been played by the hoodlums of this sleazy town—at least that's what we told ourselves until Todd showed up at the cabin out of the blue.

With him he brought good news of how we both landed a job working for his family. Apparently, we proved our loyalty by looting the shipping container, and most importantly, we didn't crack and rat them out to the cops. I hadn't worked a day in my life, the idea of work to me meant hustling commuters on Main Street

Wellington, but we were young and thinking big, lost in a banquet of opportunity.

Todd drove us to Edgecombe Street, a quiet neighbourhood two blocks down from where I slept alongside the factory generator. It was just another street where nothing appeared to happen, but just because you can't see water flowing beneath a frozen river doesn't mean nothing is happening beneath the surface.

To *work*, in Todd's world, more than likely entailed a form of illegal trade. The streets had taught me to never assume, but come-on, it's not like Todd would be getting us a job slinging off bouquets of flowers to the elderly. It had to be dealing drugs. Dealing was the most common illegal trade, everyone did it around here.

Todd parked out the front of a white weather boarded house which could be categorized somewhere in-between the lower, to middle class—the working class who only just managed to keep their heads above the water.

If anything, it didn't quite look like a drug dealers' den—but what *does* a drug dealers pad look like anyway? Maybe the picture we would paint would be of snarling pit-bulls throwing themselves at the fence as you strolled by, or an overgrown yard packed with ten or so luxurious cars that don't blend in with the house. Not to mention the endless streams of strangers dropping in for a five second catch up, day and night. But not Todd's mum's house. Instead of cars piled up in the driveway there were toy cars scattered around the driveway, and instead of a gang of thugs chilling in the yard there were toy soldiers guarding the fortress.

'Close the gate behind you,' Todd said. 'My kid brother has an eagle eye for mischief.'

A toddler in diapers stormed around the corner, intent on tackling us to the ground. He had these enormous blue eyes with a blond mullet trickling down the back of his neck. He bounced off Todd's knees as he tried to tackle him and growled at him like a gremlin—presumably, his way of saying hello. Todd scooped him up. The kid rested his head on Todd's shoulder, sucking his thumb.

'Alright there, buddy,' said Todd tenderly in a tone he seldom used. 'Let's take you inside to see mum, you must be hungry. Guys, follow me.' We bypassed the front door and went through the back patio instead. The front door was off limits and reserved for strangers only. It was a way of distinguishing friends from foes.

The kitchen was clean and orderly. Todd's mum, Jacklyn, a forty-year-old who dressed in clothes that were a bit too young for her, pulled a tray of cookies out of the oven and let them cool on the stove top. And here I was expecting to walk into a wreckage, but to my surprise this place felt and looked like a home.

Jacklyn had a peculiar look about her. Everything about her seemed to be orientated around darkness, whether it was her hair, her clothes, her heart and soul. The interior of the house had a Pagan/Wiccan theme, pentacles were hung above each doorway—later I'd discover Jacklyn swore it was a form of protection against evil spirits.

122

She was an abstractly superstitious woman, by abstracted, I mean she spoke about the universe in the same way a crazed Christian would about God, yet she persecuted any other forms of spirituality.

'You must be Tony and Corey,' she said, washing her hands in the sink. 'Take a seat, I'll be with you in a sec.' She gestured to the stalls in front of the breakfast bar.

'Mommy! Cookies!' the kid exclaimed.

'Yes, Amos,' said Jacklyn. 'You can have one once they cool down, love. Todd, honey, could you put him in his highchair and throw a bib on him—I don't want to have to wash his shirt again—by the way, I'm Jacklyn.' She placed a plate of cookies in front of us. 'Is there anything I can get you boys? Coffee, tea—a joint, or a line?'

'Joint would be good, thanks,' said Tony.

I nudged him in the ribs, shaking my head. I figured we'd be better off going into the meeting sober, no matter how casual it appeared.

Jacklyn smiled at our subtle dispute. 'Before you sell it, I think it would be wise to smoke it. This way you'll understand why it's one of the most sort out strands in the Wellington region.'

'I'm in,' Tony blurted, flashing a goofy smile. 'Corey don't smoke, but I'll definitely smoke his portion and explain every detail to him, believe me.' He uttered a dry laugh.

'It's your funeral,' said Jacklyn.

'My funeral?' Tony said. 'Jeez, my first smoke wasn't yesterday Mrs. Todd's mum—I'll tell you that much.'

'Shut that sweet little mouth and smoke it, you'll see—and its *Miss* Todd's mum.' She grinned at Tony; her smile made me feel slightly uncomfortable. 'Anyway, as you can probably tell, family is my life. I live to serve those who I consider to be family, and I expect the same in return.' She shifted her attention to Amos. He shoved as many cookies as he could into his mouth, smirking at his mum like he was the luckiest kid on the planet. 'Loyalty is what keeps me sane, and loyalty is what you proved to me after the tool exchange the other night. You're probably wondering about your payment, well, this is it.' She gestured to herself and the door we walked through. 'As Todd briefly touched on, your payment is an opportunity unlike any other, a job offering not only financial security, but protection and family. So, the question is, are you willing to be a part of *my* family?'

'Of course,' Tony replied as he exhaled. His eyes were already severely blood shot.

'Yeah,' I said, nodding.

Her dark eyes stuck to us like blackberry thorns. 'Very well,' she said, almost without emotion. 'Obviously, there's no contracts to sign, all I require of you is your word.'

'And *that* you have,' said Tony.

'Thanks, Tony, but in my world, talk is cheap, actions speak louder and paint long lasting portraits of people.'

'We won't let you down,' I said.

'I hope not. For your sake…'

A teenage girl strolled into the kitchen. She helped herself to a vodka cruiser and hovered by Jacklyn's side, seemingly standing in her shadow. Something was off with her, she wasn't all there, like her mind was on the other side of town, but somehow, she was present with us. Come to think about it, she looked like a mirror image of Jacklyn if she was half her age.

Maybe her daughter, I thought.

Like Jacklyn, her dress code was black, categorically coming off as Gothic. She looked sixteen, maybe eighteen for a push with all her make-up on. Although, her mannerisms suggested she was a teenager, her body language was awkwardly tense as if she were yet to come to terms with herself. She finished her drink. Jacklyn got her another, and she fiendishly gulped it down as if being sober was last year's craze.

'This is Charlie,' said Jacklyn.

'My real name's Miranda, though,' the girl chimed in the background.

'But she changed her name to Charlie—and for a good reason,' said Jacklyn widening her eyes, as if to say she was a speed freak.

Jacklyn stroked Charlie's lower back like she was a cat, giving her a little pat on the bottom. A heavy awkwardness lingered on our shoulders as Jacklyn glared at Charlie with the same bemused smile a kid would have for a new toy. I felt sick to my stomach, and I still don't entirely know why. But something wasn't right. Clearly Todd knew what was up by the way he rolled his eyes, turning his back on his mum as he flicked through serial brochures on the kitchen counter.

Charlie laughed forcibly, a useless attempt to expel

unwanted attention. She folded her arms over her petite chest, like she wished to build a wall of energy between us. 'I'm going to go put something warmer on,' she said.

'Off you go then,' said Jacklyn, 'I'll deal with you later.'

Charlie disappeared into Jacklyn's room where she remained until the drugs wore off. I pinned her down as a sixteen-year-old girl who made the foolish mistake of mingling with the wrong crowd. Someone who had been wronged too many times by the ones who were supposed to make us feel safe, so she made a series of mistakes which led her to this place and was yet to discover she was in the process of making yet another mistake. For some strange reason I felt close to her. I barely knew her, yet I felt like we were one in the same, hooked into a like-minded means of naivety which can only spring from a young mind, oblivious to the power of the present moment, the creative force in us all that rolls downhill, taking pieces of everything in its path.

I knew when her time would come Charlie would stare into the mirror and wonder: *who is this person staring back at me*. She'll be eighteen and somehow feels like she's forty, crucified by life's choices and the defining forces of the past. Just look at me now, I've just signed up to the drug trade for god-sake. Like the stars above, my past has influenced these choices I've made today. If I had a clean slate, all of *this* would cease to exist, who knows, I could have been some twenty-year-old rugby player with a scholarship, the potentials are infinite. But that's not the case. What matters is Charlie's just like me, only smaller, just like the hundreds of thousands of other lost souls, trying to find their way back home. Unfortunately for some, the only way home is a rope and a lack of oxygen.

***

We followed Todd to the garage, I later learned Jacklyn's home was off limits, grunts like us were only welcome when we were summoned. A white Pitbull with a black patch over one eye went off like a firework when it saw me and Tony. Its bark was so gruesome, if we weren't with Todd, he would have used our bones as chew toys.

'Don't mind him,' said Todd, snapping his fingers at the dog. 'Chief takes a while to warm up to strangers.'

We dodged the beast and entered a ram-shackled tin-house, which looked like something a drunk builder had thrown together one weekend. In the garage we found Todd's oasis. Dusty couches were laid out in an L shape, hanging onto each other by a thread in front of a TV. The couches looked like someone had dowsed them in gasoline and sent it to hell and back. There was no carpet on the floor only cold, chipped concrete. There was a predominate stench of smoke lingering in the air, infused with what I could only put down as dirty socks stuffed in the walls—even the fraying ply walls were a grungy yellow.

The windows were boarded up leaving no room for any kind of natural light. There was only one fluorescent lightbulb hanging from a cord at the centre of the garage which flickered on and off. Todd's layer was a depressing space where tomorrow would go by unnoticed.

Nailed into the crooked ply walls were a handful of Nazi propaganda posters. Hanging on the opposite wall, beside the dartboard, was a portrait of a Nazi eagle holding the Swastika in its claws. The portrait was concealed within a glass frame, quietly immortalizing the notions as it collected dust in the ominous shadows of the garage.

I noticed broken photo-frames lying on the floor. I bent over, brushed off the shards of glass and blew off the dust. Above the shattered photo-frame was a dent in the wall the size of a fist. Maybe after a couple of drinks there was a hint of resentment leaking out of Todd's abused unconscious. In the photo was a skinhead who sort of looked like Todd. The guy was saluting a child, who smiled innocently. I shrugged it off, carelessly dropping the photo-frame back to the ground like the way I found it.

'The photo's of me and my uncle Stretch,' said Todd.

'You look so young,' I said. 'He looks like you.'

Todd scrunched up his face. 'Looks are about as close as we get to any connection. He practically raised me, took on a fatherly role after my old man bailed on my mum. We used to have tinnie houses all over Upper Hutt. The cash surged through in waves, just like the paranoia. People drove all the way out from Waikanae, just to try our shit. It became an urban legend of some kind. But the money and power went straight to my uncle's head. My mum told him it was bad news written all over, but he just told her to lay off the pipe. But mum only saw what we all saw, a cell he'd eventually call his coffin.'

'Jesus,' I murmured.

'That's just the name of the game,' said Todd. 'Sometimes I feel sad when I think of him all caged like an animal, and sometimes I think it's for his own good. Uncle Stretch was too wild—too loose, so the system nailed him back into place. But they know it—and I know it, he'll never be the nail society needs to help hold the world together. So, in prison he'll rot. Some life, huh? The only memories I have of uncle Stretch revolve around fear.'

'What do you mean?' I asked.

Todd stared at the photograph as the reel of the past began to spin. 'I remember I came home from school one day all bloodied up. The bigger kids got me good that day. I ran straight to my uncle, wanting him to pick me up, and tell me everything was going to be okay...' He drifted further away, his eyes flickering. 'But nothing was okay about that day, nothings ever okay with my uncle. He beat the living shit outta me and then said, *"Boy, look in the mirror and take a good look at what I just did to you... that's exactly what I want you to do to them!"* '

'Did you?'

'Sure I did. What other choice did I have? He'd just keep beating the sense into me until I learned.' Todd peered at the boarded-up windows reflectively. 'You know, I reckon kids are like tape recorders to their surroundings, they'll always playback to you what they see, hear, and feel. The thing is, nowadays, everyone's so full of shit, we've learned to record everything that's irrelevant to our growth as a person.'

'If we played back your recording of the world, what would it sound like—the past aside, though,' I asked.

He seemed to find my question amusing. 'Take a good hard look at me, then come back to me, and you can tell me what my recording would sound like.'

'But if we are like tape recorders, we can overwrite the past, it's never too late,' I said.

'Well, aren't you a good Christian boy, Corey,' said Tony from the couch. A bunch of empty beer bottles stood on the table in front of him. He wasted no time and helped himself to the fridge. 'Allow me to remind you where we are. We're in Batman's cave, and guess what? You're Robin, I'm Robin, the only twist is, we're the villains. So cut this optimistic shit!'

Todd turned back to me. 'You see,' he said. 'What you just said is the kind of bullshit our generation have been force fed. False hope with *Disney* happy endings. Tony may not be coherent, but his statement is.'

I then decided to keep my mouth shut.

In the corner of the garage was a grubby mattress with no sheets, the pillows were just as unfulfilling. Another mattress lay in the opposite corner with what looked like fourteen-year-old puke down the side. Again, no sheets, or pillowcases. The mattresses looked like Todd had scored them from an alley down the street, not quite good enough to make it to the good-will. I've slept on pieces of cardboard that were more appetizing.

'This is where you'll be sleeping,' said Todd, pointing

130

at the mattresses contemptuously. The faint glow of the overhead lightbulb, the only source of light in the dungeon-like garage, revealed the guts of one of the mattresses, possibly torn open with a knife. Wayward springs sprung out in awkward places, certainly making for an interesting nights rest.

'You've got to be joking, mate,' said Tony. He grimaced, slamming his beer bottle on the table, and looked around the garage a second time round, this time without glitter in his eyes.

'No,' said Todd. 'If you decide to stay on a weekly basis, rent will be deducted from your wage.' Todd put a cigarette in his mouth, patting his leather jacket down for a lighter. 'I'll be staying in the next room if you need me. Bathroom's around the corner, no hot water.' He lit his cigarette and smiled gravely. 'I'll give you guys some time to settle in.'

He turned to leave.

Tony stumbled to his feet and went for the fridge and snatched two more lagers before sinking into the shredded couch.

'And Tony,' Todd said over his shoulder, 'those beers aren't complementary.' He slammed the door behind him like it were a prison cell.

'I don't know about you,' said Tony, 'but I'm going back to Joanna's for the night.'

'We don't have a choice,' I replied. 'Our first job is tomorrow.'

'Fuck this. I'm out. Joanna's got hot chow waiting for us at home.'

'Home?' I said. 'And when did Joanna's become *home*?'

He leaned in close to me; I felt his cold breath on my face. 'It's sure as hell the closest thing I've had to a home in a long time. I'm sure the same can be said for you.'

Tony went for the back door.

'I wouldn't do that if I was you,' I said. 'Chief looked pretty hungry if you ask me…'

'Fuck,' Tony murmured, ambivalently lingering around the door. Not too long after he gave up and dropped like a corpse to the mattress with loose springs.

Chapter 12

Early the next morning, I awoke to the monotonous humming of an electric razor. The mere sight of Todd casting his shadow over me, fully equipped with clippers, a blade for shaving—and for some reason unknown to me a box of matches—acted as a good substitute for a morning coffee.

'Get up you sacksa shit,' he grumbled. 'It's time you boys get tidied up.' He peeled off his black beanie, gliding his hand over his prickly scalp.

He turned his back on me and stood over Tony, grinning menacingly. It was then I noticed a horrible scar on the back of his neck. But it wasn't a scar from some type of accident—at first glance it could be perceived in this way, but if you looked closer, you'd be able to tell it was intentional, like he had been branded. Carved into the back of his neck was a poorly constructed Swastika. It was large enough to lose yourself in if you were caught in a line at your local burger joint. The lines were thick and rounded off at the ends, as if it had been infected more than a few times. Todd caught me eyeballing his scar and swiftly covered up with his beanie.

'There's no way in hell you're cutting my hair,' Tony muttered drowsily, rising crookedly from his slumber. 'I heard about what you and your pals did to that fifteen-year-old kid at Ty's birthday party.'

'Bullshit,' Todd snapped. 'That never happened.'

'My ass it never happened,' Tony replied sharply, stretching for the ceiling as his back clicked audibly.

'Well then, you boys are in luck. My old lady just happens to be an ex-hairdresser. She can make you fellas *real* pretty.'

'Yeah, glamorous,' Tony spat. 'Anything's better than looking like a ball-headed prick with a target on his head.'

'Aren't you precious this morning,' said Todd, fixing his beanie. 'It's too early in the morning for this princess act, shut up, and get your ass to the kitchen, mums waiting.'

We pulled ourselves out of our rotten beds, following his orders, but not without Tony stirring the pot. 'Are you for real with this Neo-Nazi shit?' he asked, throwing on whatever clothes were nearest to him. 'You are aware New Zealand's a multi-cultural society. As long as the Islanders keep hopping off the boat, fresher than that shaved head of yours, you'll be outnumbered, always.' Tony put his hands up, as if saying *forgive me for my truth*. 'I'm just saying, seems kinda pointless don't you think? But hey, who am I to pass judgment… I'm just another filthy rat going the wrong way in the race.'

'You done?' Todd asked calmly. Surprisingly enough, he seemed hardly phased by Tony's undesired insights. 'I've got my reasons for believing in what I do, just like you've got your reasons for selling my drugs.'

'Fair call, amigo,' said Tony, now fully dressed, but nestling back into his sleeping bag.

'Do you think I woke you guys up for my own amusement? Get the fuck up, my mum wants you in the kitchen, asap!'

After multiple moans we scuffled over the freezing concrete floor, and over the frosty grass in the backyard, where not even Chief was up to catch the morning sun. I've slept rough in alleys with broken drainage pipes leaking onto my head, but those musty mattresses win the medal for the worst sleep.

In the kitchen, Jacklyn leaned on the counter blowing into a cup of coffee. Her shoulders were slightly hunched, stiffened by the spell of the morning. She was without make-up and for once looked her age. I could see the years festering away at her bones. In spite of the clothes she wore and the many masks she painted on, behind her tight black denims hugging her thighs and waist, I could see her for what she was, a hag, a witch, who wanted no more than to be the object of peoples desires.

Two more cups of black coffee were left out for us on the breakfast bar. We looked just as bad as she did, if not worse. Our feral overgrown hair stuck out rebelliously in all different places, I for one could smell myself (Joanna hadn't the opportunity to throw my clothes in the wash for a quick cycle).

'Alright. Which one of you is first,' said Jacklyn, gesturing to the stall placed at the centre of the kitchen. Beneath the stall were sheets of yesterday's newspaper spread over the floor. In her hand she gripped a large pair of scissors. 'You can think again if your gonna go selling our finest products looking like a pile of shit a hobo left behind,' she said, pointing with the scissors at Tony. She grabbed Tony by his collar and forced him into the wooden chair. 'Don't look so worried, doll. I'll tidy you up so good, Corey over here will have to peel the girls off you.'

Once we were both trimmed and groomed, we looked like white-trash thugs who were auditioning for a boy band. She then handed us two bundles of clothing. I guess she was serious when she said a hobo's shit looked better than us. I slipped into a fresh pair of navy-blue Levi's, and threw on a leather jacket, creased in places like an old man's face. Todd's uncle Stretch came to mind. Once upon a time, it might have been his, I thought. Todd threw a shoe box at me in which I caught. Inside, there were clunky leather boots, resembling safety boots for work.

'Safety first!' Tony chimed, punching the air.

In Tony's bundle he had a similar attire of clothing. Black jeans with hard wearing leather boots, a plain black hoodie withholding that new smell which hits your nostrils when you enter a mall. Instead of leather, he was given a faded sky-blue denim jacket, torn in places under the arms and down the sides, like the previous owner got into a knife fight. On the side of either shoulder was an iron-on patch from nineties rock bands. 'Hey, Cor,' Tony said in a tone drenched with sarcasm. 'Check me out, I'm a rock guy.' He formed the devil horns with his hand, holding it up to the ceiling like he intended on defying the ten commandments as well as attending a Jona's Brothers concert.

Jacklyn put her hands to her hips, evaluating her creations. 'Not bad,' she said. 'Charlie! Get those sweet cheeks out here, I need your two-sense!'

Charlie poked her head out of Jacklyn's bedroom, her eyes heavy with sleep, with nothing but a bed sheet wrapped around her body. In the morning light I could tell it wasn't her natural hair colour. Her hair was black, like Jacklyn's, although her hair did not match her green eyes. I could tell Charlie wanted to say something like, *I didn't know Justin Bieber was a hobo*. Or something else full of cheek. But instead, she nodded timidly, standing in awkward display between the door frame, nodding her head. So it seemed she had grown comfortable with being a fly on the wall, this way, she couldn't be swatted by the nastiness which poured out of the mouths of insecurity—and for a young and emerging girl, like Charlie, there were a lot of unpleasant words flying out of broken people's mouths, like venomous acid searing through self-esteem.

'Do they tick all the right boxes?' Jacklyn asked Charlie. 'Tonight they're off for their first job with Todd.'

'Yeah,' she said. 'You guys look good.'

'Alrighty,' Jacklyn said, clasping her hands together.

'Follow me, it's time you get to know our *system*.'

We followed Jacklyn through the lounge, careful not to trip on the Lego towers built at knee level (as high as Amos could build them). The television was flashing morning cartoons at a deafening volume, Amos sat on the caramel-coloured carpet in front of the telly, dressed in pyjamas with red cars all over it. The fireplace was blasting away in the corner, quietly devouring chunks of pine. For a boy like Amos this was his sanctuary, his world of lovingly comforts. However, in twenty years' time I'd like to check up on him to see the kind of man he had become.

Jacklyn cold shouldered her son, her eyes glowing with determination. This was a matter of business, a means to keep that fireplace warming up the house, a way to pay for those pyjamas warming up her son's little body. This was an occupation, as unorthodox as it was it provided income. There was no place for three-year-old boys in this portion of his mother's world, only for those who were old enough to sell their soul.

Down a hall with creaky wooden floorboards was a broad white door Jacklyn unlocked with a set of keys she fished out of her buxom back pocket. Behind the door was a cheap looking desk with two computer screens facing some geek who frantically tapped his mouse with one hand, the other crunched a big can of Red Bull, which he discarded in the bin beside him. The spotty faced geek glanced up at us, then jolted back in his office chair in fright. 'Jesus!' he exclaimed. 'You scared the shit outta me! Could you care as much to knock next time?' I noticed his belt was undone. He quickly did it up, terminating multiple tabs on the computer screen to the left.

'Sometimes you really make me wonder, Clark,' said Jacklyn, sniffing the air. The tiny office stunk of body odour, sugary drinks, and... I'll leave that one for you to decide.

His blemished face flushed, amplifying acne scars beneath his cheeks. He followed our eyes to his belt. 'I had stomach pains,' he protested, patting his belly which sagged ever so slightly over his leather belt.

'Whether it was all those energy drinks or—' Jacklyn lost herself a moment. '—whatever you are doing, it needs to stop, okay. We need your focus, without it, I have no jobs, without jobs we lose all of *this*.'

Clark readjusted his moon shaped glasses. 'Yes, mam,' he muttered, like a teenager who just received a lecture.

'These are our new recruits, Corey and Tony. They'll be filling in for Josh and Shaun—'

'What happened to Josh and Shaun?' Clark asked.

Jacklyn didn't blink. 'We had to let them go...'

'Well then, on that note,' Clark said, swinging around in his chair, holding out a clammy hand. 'Nice to meet you. I'm Clark, the hacker.'

Neither of us shook his hand. Tony and I studied his grubby palm with high brows. Clark smiled painfully, wiping his hand on his trousers. 'Okay, the system...' He pondered his computer a moment, before pulling up Facebook on his right screen. 'Well, basically, using my

intuitive knowing's, along with ninja hacking abilities—
and with a pinch of charm—'

'Just get to the point already!' snapped Jacklyn.

Clark uttered an awful sound from his nasal passage,
snorting hideously, until it sort of resembled that of a
freakish laugh. 'I've created a God-like search engine,
granting me access to whomever, and whatever sparks
light to my frontal cortex.' He leaned back in his chair,
put his hands behind his head, and smiled to himself,
peering sightlessly into a world where live cam-girls
thought keyboard warriors were desirable. 'I've infiltrated
Facebook's privacy defence, thus granting me direct
access to just about anyone's personal information. This
is for strictly 'business'…' His voice cracked, going from
a forced calmness to a jittery defensive dweeb. 'For the
record I'm no stalker. I only use this power in a formal
sense, I never overexert it, never…'

Tony puckered his lips, widened his eyes, and
exchanged glances with me and nodded slowly. I smirked
at him, subtly shaking my head from side to side as Clark
rambled on. 'Using the modified search engine, I can
access the infinite by typing in 'keywords' that will filter
through undesired information. Its gold we're after
gentlemen, so we've got to shake up the bowl to rid
ourselves of everything brittle and rocky. For instance,
let's say, I'll search, 'harassment'. Then I'll receive every
comment, every private message, orientated around that
word.' Again, Clark leaned back into his chair, putting his
hands on-top of his head which looked like a greasy mop
head. 'But this is less specific. To gain customers, fast, we

need to be more concise. This means a target audience needs to be generated. You follow me homies?'

'Yeah, I get you,' I said.

Tony folded his arms, looking unamused.

'So, in terms of the drug trade, I'll search: *Parties Hutt Valley*.' He read it out loud as he frantically typed and pressed enter. Flashing on the screen was every scheduled party in our area, including addresses, individual profiles of those who were attending, right down to the total number of guests. 'Through this information I can form an estimate on the potential for profits. It's a matter of filtering out those who don't match our *criteria*. There you have it, gentlemen, customers who don't even know they are predestined to buy a bag of pot off some jerks' friend of a friend, you get me? Because they don't know you but—'

'Yeah, we get the joke,' Tony said bluntly.

'Give me two hours,' Clark said, 'then I'll have your first job set up for you.' He gave us the thumbs up. 'Any questions?'

'No,' Tony and I said.

'Cool bananas!' said Clark. 'Once I finish up here, Jacklyn will hand over the nights inventory—oh, and tell her I'll give her a call once I've established the appropriate addresses.'

'Hey, Clark,' Tony said over his shoulder before we exited. 'There's absolutely nothing cool about bananas. . . just thought you should know.'

***

For the rest of the afternoon, we lounged around the garage. Gradually, over time, handfuls of cigarette butts formed at our feet, as we nervously waited for the call from Jacklyn.

'Have you heard from Joanna?' I asked Tony.

'Nah, I haven't,' he said. 'That's the thing, I should've…' He ran his dirty fingernails through his freshly clipped red hair, the dirt still trapped under his nails from when we scrambled up the flooded creek-bed. 'Makes me wonder if her old man did something to her—'

'Don't say that. He's probably just taken her phone.'

'I hope you're right,' Tony said soberly.

The back door to the garage screeched open, sending shivers down my spine. Todd, I thought. He's the only one who'd make it across the backyard by himself without getting mauled by Chief. Sure enough it was him. Dressed in his usual apparel, a leather jacket pulled over a hoodie, ripped denims, and a black beanie covering his skeletal head. His face tiresome, cold with no emotion. No affection received; no affection displayed. But this was just Todd—or at least how I had come to know him.

'Our ride's outside,' he muttered with a flicker of agitation. 'Get a move on. I'll be accompanying you for the night.'

'What for?' I asked.

He froze for a second, watching a cockroach scale the wall, heading in the path of a spider's web. 'Moral support,' he said finally. 'I'll be your iron shield.'

'Where are you taking us?' Tony asked.

We shared an uneasy silence as he watched the cockroach walk right into the web.

'Pomare,' he said.

Chapter 13

I was holding roughly half an ounce in the secret compartment of my jacket pocket. Tony had the other half in a leather pouch. Jacklyn and Todd divided the weed into individual baggies, one baggie consisting of two grams went for twenty-five bucks a pop. Normally, she sold two grams for thirty but for tonight they were on special, Jacklyn wanted to gain some loyal customers. 'Better to start them off young,' she said to us before we left.

It was another freezing night; the streets were empty and filled with fog. An old wagon was parked out front with its headlights on, steam poured out from beneath the bonnet as the engine hummed dismal melodies.

Resting on the bonnet with a rollie hanging out of his mouth was a person I thought I'd never see again, for their sake. I recognized his shaggy mop of brown hair, swished to the side messily, the rest of his hair running down his bony cheeks, his nose crooked like his slyness.

The way he carried himself was like a greasy used car salesman. He was nothing more than a con artist. A degenerate. It was Clinton.

'The shepherd has arrived,' he announced in his tangy, southern accent. 'Oh, and he has two meek sheep. What're your names gentlemen—wait, don't bother, where your headin' the g-bangers will put you on the block and turn your asses into mincemeat.'

'Shut your goddamn mouth, Clinton,' said Todd. 'Unlike yourself, these guys know how to keep their mouths shut… and when was the last time you saw a dentist? Shit, your teeth look like crooked shards of meth.'

Clinton's face dropped. His mouth sealed shut. He raised his middle finger defiantly at Todd, holding it dauntingly close to his face. 'Fuck you, Todd! and fuck your whore mother as well!' He blew up like an inflatable ball, then exhaled releasing his tension through one deep breath. 'Let's get this bullshit over with so I can get paid.' He turned his back and went for the driver's door.

A primitive rage overtook me. Flashbacks ran through my mind of the night he rolled me, and there he was standing before me, completely oblivious to my existence. I was the last thing on his mind. He probably screwed over more vulnerable people than he could keep up to date with. Without considering the consequences I lunged at him, taking him down to the pavement with me. I pinned his shoulders down with my knees, taking wild swings at his head.

'What the fuck is this?' he shouted, squirming on the

ground.

Clinton intended on robbing me the moment he picked me up. He stripped me of my utilities and the freedom I dreamed about every night on the streets. Perhaps I wouldn't be getting ready to sell drugs if Clinton and his buddies never intervened. But they did. Those cold-hearted bastards did. So I threw right and left blows at his face, hoping to leave a bruise or two, some kind of mark which acted as a signature for my redemption.

'Get this nut off me!' Clinton shrieked.

Tony swooped in, yanking me off by my shoulders. Todd shielded Clinton just in case I broke lose. Blood dribbled down his nose, he wiped it with his shirt sleeve and spat blood at me. 'Who's this nut?' he asked. 'Damn boy, you got some moves. Maybe next time you can give me a heads up before you wanna brawl. Then we'll see who the real warrior is.' He took a step in my direction.

'Back the fuck up!' Todd yelled.

Clinton stared at me blankly, red glimmered in his eyes. 'Ah, I remember you! The tin-man bum. Blaze is still farting from all those beans you gave us—'

'You fucking stole them from me!'

Tony's grip tightened around my shoulders.

'I believe you handed them over to us,' Clinton said adamantly, so convincingly I nearly believed it myself.

'Whatever beef you two have, save it,' Todd said. 'There's a job that needs to be done. You animals can rip each other's torsos apart when we get back into Upper Hutt.'

'Fuck you! Piecea shit bum!' Clinton snarled at me. 'If it wasn't for your daddy over here, I'd have your head on a plate!'

***

The tension between us slowly dissipated as we gunned down the highway, lost in a gloomy silence. In the time it took to smoke three cigarettes we pulled into Pomare Central, a place where you drove in, and drove out—if you were not from this part of town. For us strangers it was a dangerous place, especially with someone like Todd by our side.

We took a sharp right, taking us deeper into the concrete jungle where statehouses and cheerless apartment blocks wilted in all directions, like trees which tried, but failed to grow in face of the sun. The streetlights grew dimmer and appeared to lose their reign as we drove slowly down a narrow street. Creatures of the night poked their heads out of pitch-black alleys, with caps tilted sideways, their shirts three sizes too big like their wild eyes.

'This is it,' Clinton said darkly, lining the vehicle up to the curb.

We relayed our eyes to the house of unknowable outcomes, shaken by the unruly beats resounding from the party.

'Okay, follow my lead,' said Todd, pulling his beanie over his bald head, cloaking his shiny white target. 'You got the shit?'

I patted the inner layer to my jacket pocket, nodding.

'Best wishes, ladies,' Clinton said. 'I'll keep the car running, just in case you meatheads run inta any trouble—if so, I'm not here to help, just drive.'

'Thanks for the confidence, asshole,' Tony grumbled as he unbuckled his seatbelt.

As we proceeded down the driveway, I was surprised to see the front porch unmanned. Normally at such gatherings there was a militant-like presence at the doorstep, taking on the role as the muscle of the party. Based upon the distant clinking of beer bottles, as well as the slurring speech, most of the party had migrated to the backyard.

'Do we knock?' I asked shakily.

Todd shook his head and fiddled with the doorknob. It was open.

Our presence brought upon a dry spell in conversation. Many heads turned. Thuggish caricatures sized us up, their mere look stunted the idea of any further movements. A broken cluster of girls whose jeans were bursting at the seams with youthful fullness, watched on curiously, raising their cans of drink to their red lips, taking large gulps as they too, sized us up in a different kind of way.

Most of the party looked to be a couple of years younger than us, some looked old enough to still be in high school. I watched a bunch of baby-faced youth with snap-back caps chugging down beer bongs, chanting and carrying on like the night would never end. I had seen it all before. They were the type of people who lived for the weekend, chicks, booze, and of course drugs—lots of drugs to distract them from themselves. But they didn't realize the party would come to an end—it had to at some point—and that 'lucky lady' one of the guys got with would fall pregnant to a man she'd later resent. Regretfully, the two of them would never see beyond the Hutt Valley hills. Those hills that once shielded them from the dangers of the big wide world. But in time, those hills would become a prison of trees and dirt, consolidating their once boundless horizons to a dim window of opportunity.

However exposed to the rawness of life, the party goers appeared to be limited to seeing only a fraction of life's story, a descending narrative received through a narrow telescope. As long as they stayed here confined by their violently driven ambitions, they'd die not knowing what waited for them on the other side, they'd die not knowing through choice, and through will, they held the power all along to expand the lens of their telescope.

Nobody harassed us or threw questions down our throats; it did make me wonder how many other people showed up uninvited. Or maybe little *Jimmy's* parents were away for the weekend, and he decided to impress all his high school buddies by throwing the party everyone would eventually forget.

'I'm off for a smoke,' Todd said. 'Best way to get with the people, if you know what I mean.' He pulled a joint out of his cigarette packet, giving us a wink.

'Wait,' Tony said, 'what do we do?'

'Exactly what you came here to do. Push product.'

'What? So you want us to announce to the entire party: *get ya weed, twenty- five bucks for two grams—best stuff in town folks!'* said Tony.

'No,' said Todd, amused by his naivety. 'Use your wit, your street smarts, intuit the situation and swoop on in well its hot. Remember dealing works in the same way as conversation. Conversation leads to conversation leads to conversation… catch my drift?'

'Not really,' I said.

'If you encounter trouble, what's the signal?'

I formed a symbol with my hand which resembled the east side gang sign.

'Yeah, like that's not gonna get us into any trouble in a place like this,' said Tony.

Amid Tony's doubtful ramblings, Todd faded into the crowd.

'How do we go about this?' said Tony. He was frigid and on edge, I'd never seen him like this before.

'There's some people over there who look like potential customers,' I said, nodding my head at the same group of girls who were still in awe of our presence. I leaned in close and whispered into Tony's ear, 'No one knows who we are, we're a blank canvas. Bro, we're free to be whoever we want to be, there's nobody to reinforce our sense of identity.'

This insight appeared to give his confidence a boost. 'I know what you're saying,' he said. 'It's just a party, only difference is we've got a load of drugs. It doesn't really change anything at all, does it?'

'Nah. We're just two guys looking for a good time.

We're not pushy salesman, we're the type of guys people want to hang with.'

'Yeah!' Tony boomed. 'Fuck yeah! I'm down with your vision.' Tony strolled over to the group of girls, who erected their postures once they picked up Tony had them within his sight. They were Māori or Polynesian—I can't remember specifically—brown and beautiful, eighteen and free with the world at their feet. They took an instant liking to us *older guys*, soaking in our tales of the hills and the homeless nights.

One of the girls, Jasmine, stuck to my side for the remainder of the night. She had short black hair touching the tip of her shoulders, her eyes big and brown. Jasmine wore her heart on her sleeve and openly discussed her up bringing and how her mother was always tangled in a new guy every week. Because of this, they did a lot of moving, a lot of running. Her mother had taught her it's easier to run than it is to face the source of our problems. I could see it in her eyes, she was still running, but what she was running from was unclear to me at the time.

Tony's girl, Tasha, seemed to fit into a similar category. Though, she was a bit more reserved than Jasmine. She had long, wavy black hair with sad brown eyes, and a heart of gold that had been trampled on too many times. She was distant and a bit shy. But it wasn't long until Tony broke her down with his humour and charm. He had her in hysterics for most of the night. Tony really brought Tasha out of her shell, and in no time, she was goofing about without the slightest care for people's petty judgments. Tony tended to have this effect

151

on people. They had only just met but they seemed to fit together, Tony's extroversion pulled Tasha out of her shell, and Tasha's emotional intelligence attuned Tony to his feelings in which he normally ignored.

I guess we were sort of a different breed compared to the thuggish script everyone here seemed to follow. We made our first sale to the girls with an added bonus in the bathroom. Todd must have been hinting to us the key to making sales when he disappeared out back to pass round a joint, *connect with the people, therefore, someone knows someone who knows someone.*

In less than an hour we sold out. At a party this size it didn't take long for word to go around. We slipped out back to find Todd to show him the nights earnings. Tony and I staggered out the back door, our arms loosely wrapped around our girl's shoulders. The vodkas Tasha and Jasmine provided us with stirred up an impaired blurriness, nonetheless we were happy and smoothly intoxicated.

Jasmine and Tasha floated on a similar cloud, although they were higher in the sky than I was. Jacklyn's product received the tick of approval from the customers. Everyone's swollen, dreamy eyes said it all. The more Jasmine and Tasha smoked, the more apparent their Polynesian features became, their eyes glazed over with an exotic, Asian looking haze. It was dazzling.

Tony and the girls couldn't stop hugging each other, discussing the uncanniness of the situation. Then again, they were high, and I was just tipping over the edge of Captain Morgan's ship, discovering more rummaging treasure in a box tucked beneath an unattended seat. I cracked open another can of rum and coke, heading toward the back end of the yard, where Todd was swarmed by drunkards as he established what looked like a joint rolling station where you paid as you go.

Spotting me amidst the crowd, he tugged my arm and led me to the other side of the yard, which had quickly become the sick bay for the wounded who could hardly walk or string a sentence together.

'Let's bounce,' he said, showing me his empty leather pouch. 'I'm out. Soon they'll realize and hit us like a zombie apocalypse. How'd you fellas do?'

I showed him my empty pouch. 'Fine to say the least—just take a look around, I think it says it all.'

'Perfect,' Todd replied. 'Let's get out now before some jack-off decides to jump us.'

He held out his hand. We shook firmly. 'Well done. You did a good job.'

'Oh and, Todd,' I said hesitantly. 'We made some new friends. Can they come with us?'

Todd glanced to the rear of the yard where Tony and Tasha were sticking their tongues down each other's throats. It was a sight less passionate, leaning more toward animalistic. Jasmine stood to the side of them, watching. She fixed those exotic brown eyes to me, puckering her lips subtly, beckoning me to join.

'I see that, Corey,' said Todd. 'If there's room in Clinton's backseat, I don't see why not, but we gotta go, now.'

I hailed Tony. 'We're on the move!'

Startled by just about anything that wasn't Tasha's lips, Tony stared at me with stars in his eyes. Drunk on her kisses I assumed.

Together, we walked back to the car, happy to leave the madness behind. Tony and the girls straggled behind; they were less content on the idea of leaving. I stuck with Todd who kept to himself as usual, looking like he was brewing up some deep thoughts.

'Hey Todd,' I said, 'You've gotta tell me, what's with all those Nazi posters in the garage? You're not for real about that stuff, are you?'

'The posters are my uncles, as well as the philosophies. I inherited the rest.'

'I saw the scar on the back of your neck… you always wear a beanie, if you believe in that stuff, why do you hide away from it?'

He took his time to answer. 'There was a time when my beliefs did something for me, I felt connected to something bigger than me—it was almost spiritual. But that was then… and this is now. I can't run from my past, but I can hide from it.'

'You don't need to hide from it,' I said. 'I saw you in there, man, vibing out with the people, they loved you.'

'They didn't love *me*; they loved the fact I was holding drugs. They're high, that's all. It'd be a different story if I was dry, I'll tell you that much,' he said, quick to justify.

'I beg to differ,' I replied.

We were crossing the road when Todd froze, and he leered in the direction of Clinton's car. Todd turning to stone prompted my attention, forcing me to be on guard.

It was then I saw the man sitting on the bonnet of Clinton's car who turned him into ice.

He was sharing a smoke with Clinton, slouching over his knees, but perked up when he saw us. Despite the cold, he was dressed in a wife-beater singlet tucked into blue jeans. His arms were buff, and like Todd's, covered in a mural of tattoos, except Todd's tattoos were done by artists, this guy's tattoos were more than likely made of piss and ink—the signature style of a prison job.

This man had no place in my world, the only place I recognized him was from inside a dusty photo-frame Todd had laid to waste on his garage floor. Unlike Todd, I kept walking to get a better look. The man's face was heinously creased with age, as if he had endured many battles—possibly with himself and countless foes. He was indeed the same man from the photograph, only older, and leaning toward the tubby side, prison grub mustn't be so bad after all.

'Don jus stand there, son,' Stretch boomed in a steely voice nails couldn't penetrate. 'Come shake ye uncles' hand—shit, you can hug me if ya like, if yall stilla sissy like I remember!'

Todd approached him apprehensively. After a long silence he finally managed to speak. 'I thought I'd—'

'Neva see me again?' Stretch broke in. 'Damn, that makes two of us. Let's jus say a good lawyer is all it takes to bail you outta ye rut.'

'What do ya know,' Clinton muttered. 'Even in the shittiest parts of town you run into a familiar face. I was just doin some light readin, then there was a knock on me window. It was like he fell from the sky!'

'Clinton you're still a dozy little prick, I'll tell ye that much,' said Stretch. 'You talk too much shit; some things never change. The shorter version of the story is ye mother told me where you were goin ta be. I jus happened to spot this knuckle-head from a mile away.' He jabbed Clinton in the arm. 'I hear you've got some new grunts on our team, would dis happen to be one of em?' His eyes landed on me with a death-defying thud. 'Ye better hope ta god ya pouch is empty, and those pockets eh yours are full!' Stretch croaked. 'Cos I'm in need for a boxa piss and a cheap whore!'

At last, Tony and the girls caught up to us.

'Whatawe have er? Couple of the towns finest?' said Stretch, roaring with laughter. Clinton joined in laughing like the sheep he was.

Tasha screwed up her face, as if she trampled over a spike. She grabbed Tony's hand and tried to steer him in the opposite direction.

'Come to my place,' she said, her voice passing off as a whisper. 'It's only a few blocks down.'

'What's with da sudden change in heart, love?' said Stretch. 'Aren't I as handsome as dis bloke?'

To this, Tasha gave no answer. 'Are you coming or not?' she asked, eager to depart.

Torn between clicks, Tony's face said it all. He wanted to swing with the good times with Tasha, but at the same time he was fearful of Stretches reaction.

'He's not goin anywhere with yew,' Stretch said with such hate, such malice. 'Ye bush-niggers got too many

156

diseases. The boys probably already caught somethin off of ya from you jus hangin off his arm.'

'Yup…' Clinton muttered dumbly. 'Once you got the herpes that's the end of ya. It'll stick to you for life.' He stared thoughtfully into space. 'Like knocked up ex-girlfriends and child support payments.'

Jasmine bit her tongue for as long as she could, but eventually she erupted in ever flowing curses. 'I can't believe the shit I'm hearing! Like, are you for real? Fuck you, you white piecea shit! I know people round here who'll chop off your limbs for saying shit like that!'

'Ya-ll see what I mean, boys?' said Stretch, eying me and Tony. 'Ders a native on ya tail who'll spear you any second.'

'Fuck you asshole!' Jasmine shouted. She turned to face me. 'Is this the kind of people you kick it with, Corey?'

'Jasmine,' I said, wishing to explain, but the context of the situation was too overbearing for her to hear me out. 'It's a lot more complicated than it appears.'

'Not at all!' she snapped, refusing to lower the pitch of her voice. 'Consider me dead if your gonna hang out with these kinds of people. Tasha! Come on!'

Tony gripped Tasha's hand, refusing to let her go. A game of tug of war broke out between Tony and Jasmine. Finally, Tasha ended it all. 'Get the fuck off me, Tony!' She screamed. 'Let me go!'

'Tasha, please, don't go,' Tony implored. 'It's a long story but I can explain—this is all one big misunderstanding—a mistake!'

Jasmine took a hold of Tasha's hand, leading her deeper into the shadows of the street. They vanished into the night. Not too long after, we heard Tasha's voice echo from afar. 'The only mistake I made was letting you into my life, Tony!'

Chapter 14

Most of the time our experiences in time are bland and mundane to the point of forgetting its significance. But regardless of our interpretation it shapes us into the people we are today. We gain or we lose, it can be no other way. Positive, negative, day, night, moon, sun, Yin Yang—the pinnacles of creativity.

A shared experience is all it takes to seal a bond for a lifetime. One night is all it takes. In that moment of time, you were brilliant, rebellious and bold—despite what other people would say. Tony, I remember like it was yesterday…

It all started late one Tuesday night when we were sixteen years old. Tony messaged me just as I laid my head down on my pillow.

'Wanna ride?' he said.

I responded with a question mark.

'I'll pick you up in half an hour, got my Gran's car…'

By this time, my foster parents were fast asleep in bed, dead to the world for the next nine hours. I slipped out the back door, leaving it unlocked. I ventured out into the deserted streets lit only by the stars above. Parked a few houses down was a wee Honda hatchback, the kind of car you'd expect to see a pensioner drive. Tony gave the horn a friendly honk and flashed the lights at me.

'I can't believe you actually stole your Gran's car,' I said, jumping into the front seat.

'Well, believe it,' said Tony. 'Where do you wanna go?'

'As far away from this shit-hole town as possible,' I said.

He ignited the ignition and revved up the old girl mockingly— probably the most action the car had seen in a decade. Tony glanced at the fuel gage. 'I can take you as far as Upper Hutt and back, so maybe we'll have to leave the road trip for another time.'

'Good enough for me,' I said.

He shifted gear and blitzed out the mouth of the valley. On the highway he pushed the hatchback to its limits, the car groaned as he put his foot down, climbing up to speeds of 120 and beyond. The car had probably only ever seen a steady speed of 50 its entire existence.

The roads were dead quiet, the only sign of life came from the golden arches of McDonald's and various gas stations as we powered into Silverstream.

'Dude, want to go for a drive into the school?' Tony asked, a mischievous smile growing on his face.

'Yeah, let's do it,' I said.

We both howled with laughter, already eager to unload our nightly voyage to our mates at school. But the story wouldn't be complete without wreaking havoc on the school's famous grounds which they took so much pride in.

To our surprise the elegant spear ended gate pillars were left open. Tony pulled in and brought the vehicle down in speed, stealthily cruising over the speed bumps as we edged closer into the gloom of the courtyard. The deeper we drove, the narrower our way of passage became. Lucky for us the hatchback slid through the gaps like a cockroach trudging in the shadows.

Tony switched the head lights to high beam, illuminating the old cobble stone walls, and the red brick laid walls towering into the night sky around us. He idled the car down a strip of asphalt the width of an alley way, which acted as a shortcut past the auditorium. The path opened as we neared the borders lodge.

My heart thumped. My anxiety shifted into rapid flowing adrenaline. Tony turned to me; his face silhouetted by the overhanging shadows leaning off the building.

'Should I?' he asked. He had this look in his eye as if he had already made up his mind but was looking for moral support.

I laughed awkwardly, and gave a vague nod of the head, not knowing what he had in mind, but willing to ride out the consequences, whatever they would be. He shifted gears, pounding his foot on the accelerator. The tires swirled and the engine hissed, smoke rose from beneath the tires filling the air with black smoke. One by one, the lights switched on in the border's rooms like a luminous domino sequence. He hurriedly put the car into drive and steered the old girl back to the entrance of the school.

I expected him to make a dash onto the freedom of Ferguson drive, heading north as far as half a tank of gas would take us. Instead, Tony accelerated over the curb and drove onto the prestige school grounds—a place well regarded by the school and the public who passed it by. The lawns were mowed weekly, and the gardens were attended to daily, yet soon enough, once Tony was done, they'd have their work cut out for them.

He thrashed the car around, carelessly pulling up the handbrake as he savagely spun the steering wheel around, ripping up the lush green grass, leaving behind jagged tire marks which looked like hideous earthy scars. He swung the car around to the face of the school and mounted the curb, causing our seatbelts to cease as we jerked forward unexpectedly.

'I've always wanted to do that,' said Tony, bobbing up and down in the driver's seat.

Once we reached a safe distance Tony pulled over. This time I took the wheel. I put my foot down hard and glanced in-between the speedometer, zipping my eyes between the road and the rising speed. We were going 120 down a 50k zone, running red lights, whooshing through the drowsy residential suburbs of Upper Hutt, going too fast to think of stopping.

This went on for some time until the artificial glow of the city centre seeped into my tunnel vision. I eased on the brakes and took a sharp right going around the city to avoid any unwanted surprises.

My hands began to tremble from the mixture of adrenaline and general fear, so I pulled over opposite the railway tracks to let Tony drive the rest of the way.

'I'll do one more burn out, then I'll drop you home, got to get the car back to my Gran before she finds out,' he said, glancing at the time.

Looking back, we should have really left then and there, maybe then, the path laid out before us would disintegrate and allow another potential future to form. But it didn't.

Tony found a wide street with plenty of room to tear up the asphalt. We were riding steadily, then suddenly, the engine choked, roaring hatefully at skyrocketing speeds. Tony gripped the wheel with all his mite, his expression cemented in concentration. He tugged on the handbrake and attempted to swerve the car around in a circular motion. But we were going too fast. Despite Tony's frantic manoeuvre's it was useless, the car drifted along the road like it had *been caught in some gravitational rip. It happened all too fast; all I could do was brace myself for the unknown. The car skidded straight into a lamppost with a vicious thud. Blank faced, we gazed at one another, consumed by the airy sounds of defeat. It was in this moment, within this experience, together, we began to spiral down in paradise.*

Chapter 15

We were almost in Upper Hutt, riding in the backseat with Stretch at the wheel, Clinton up front, and us boys squashed in the back. I was worried about Tony. He was still beat up over what Tasha had said to him. As for myself, I didn't care too much for ditching the girls, through my experience girls required too much attention, attention I didn't have and wasn't willing to give. They were like flowers needing to be nurtured, otherwise the relationship would wilt, dry up, and die.

He didn't speak or form eye contact with anyone on the journey *home*. His face withheld the angst of rejection, silently suffering as he peered down at his feet, ignoring the scenes of the suburban night, alive with wailing police sirens, senseless fist fights, and drunken brawls over wounded egos.

Something was seriously wrong with him. He looked beaten down by the hands of desolation. His disconnection was a sure sign of rejection. I too had experienced rejection, if not that night, but enough to understand it like a friend.

Stretch dominated the conversation, reciting the wisdom he obtained in prison. Clinton seemed to be the only one who paid any attention. It turned out Tony was beat-up over Tasha, but this was merely salt in the wound. I studied Tony's eyes while thinking: *these vicious streets… these empty shells of heartless people, kicking us while we're already down, but they didn't care, nobody cared for anything other than themselves. If he wanted, Tony could pull himself to his feet. But he knew in time someone would beat him down again. Oh, these streets, sheltering these depraved, broken people… we're all down on the grit of the pavement, beaten too many times, until we no longer feel pain at all…*

It was hard to see Tony like this with the life drained out of him. It wasn't the person I had come to know since we were kids.

'Don't worry about it,' I said quietly, careful to not provoke Stretches attention. However, Stretch was too self-indulgent to know any different. Todd, on the other hand tuned in, curious to know why Tony came down so abruptly.

'She's just a girl,' I continued to say, 'there's plenty more of them.'

'It's not just about Tasha!' he snapped.

Stretched craned his neck around to the backseat. 'You'll get ye money, ranga. Then ye can buy yeself a girl ten times more cut out than ye bush-girl!' Stretch cackled, whacking the back of Clinton's hollow head.

'We'll talk about it when we get home,' I said.

165

'Home?' asked Tony, laughing sarcastically. 'What does that even mean?'

I myself didn't know. But it was a place with shelter and grub, so it had to be a home.

Once Stretch had called us soft-cocks at least two times each, we pulled into Edgecombe Street. Jacklyn was waiting in the kitchen, a glass pipe lay on the table beside her mug of tea, she puffed on it reflectively, counting the money.

'All right,' she said, 'here's your earnings—grunts normally get paid last, but just for tonight seeing you boys did a good job, here's your cut.' She handed us each a small bundle of green bills. It might have been from all the movies I watched, but I expected to receive a little more than we did. Jacklyn sensed my dissatisfaction. 'You were just selling weed, doll,' she said in a motherly tone. 'If you wanna chase higher dollars you'll have to dive into the A-class scene… but then again, you have to be willing to lose in order to gain—sometimes the price you pay will be your freedom.'

Ideally, Tony and I both wanted fast money. We didn't plan on sticking around for very long, we just wanted enough cash to keep us afloat until we figured out our next move.

I watched Jacklyn hover a lighter beneath her glass pipe, taking rapid puffs. 'So…' she blurted out between breaths. 'Is there anything else I can help you with, or are you two just gonna stand and stare?'

'What are the chances of us dealing some stronger stuff?' I asked.

She laughed. 'Already catching the money bug, huh? I'll look into it, honey. But for now, you boys need to get outta my kitchen.'

***

We lit half a dozen candles switching off the lights as the garage fell into a miserable silence. In the dimness of the candlelight, we pushed our mattresses together so we felt closer (with the light off we felt a world away). Dressed in the same clothes from the party, we pulled our hoods up and nestled into our sleeping-bags.

'So, are you gonna tell me what's up?' I asked.

'I can't deal with my own fuckin' life,' said Tony. 'I can't love. I can't *be* loved, I don't know how to receive it. All I ever do is hurt myself and other people.' He covered his eyes with his hands, rubbing them as if trying to refine his vision. 'You're on a similar wave, Corey. I guess that's why we crossed paths. There's no place for us in this world... no matter how hard we try something is always stopping us from reaching the happiness every person deserves.' He grimaced, holding his hand out to the floor as he felt around for a bottle of beer that wasn't there. 'Just look what happened to us at the party. Did you see the sparkle in Tasha and Jasmine's eyes when they were around us? They genuinely enjoyed our company—they pretty much invited us back to their place to lay down with them for god sake! But like what happened at Joanna's we were denied. There was no chance to be a part of a greater whole... love offered but

167

our hands were tied behind our backs.'

'The Tasha and Jasmine thing was purely circumstantial,' I protested. 'They didn't know the full story to why we were hanging around hillbillies and skinheads!'

'Bullshit, Corey,' said Tony stonily. 'You can keep telling yourself that, but I know for a fact it's not true.'

I didn't know what to say. Maybe Tony was right, and I was just blind. I normally had a way with words, a gift to make people feel better, but tonight I was not to be the optimistic light at the end of the tunnel. I was the uncertainty that comes with not knowing if the despair would come to an end. Maybe, after all, I am all but the false hope of that light, the light that would flirt with our eyes, but never come our way.

'You're not alone, bro,' I said. 'We've got each other... and never forget that, regardless of how bad things get. I love you like a brother. We've been through too much, side by side, for anything, or anyone, to come in the way of our friendship. You'll always be a part of my story—and always will be, whether you choose to stay or go someplace different. You've left an impression on my soul; thanks to you I no longer feel alone...'

We drifted away with these feelings, falling into the arms of sleep. Tony rested his head on my words, and for once, so did I.

Chapter 16

Early the next morning I had to drag Tony out of bed by his ankles. I had a pocketful of money and visions of bacon, eggs and coffee. I couldn't wait to go out and pay someone to cook me breakfast. Yes, me, Corey Gnosis, aka the tin-man bum.

'Wakey wakey!' I said to Tony, hovering my money around his nose. 'We're going out!'

Tony looked unwell, his face a ghostly white. 'Water,' he managed to mumble after much effort.

His condition was severe, so I rushed to the other side of the garage, slipping out the door which led to Todd's quarters. I returned with a glass of rusty water and Tony guzzled it down in a matter of seconds. The colour slowly returned to his face, but his eyes were still blood-shot and glassy.

'All right,' said Tony, pressing his fingers to his clammy forehead. He looked like he was rocking on a boat, about to pop with puke. 'Let's get your bacon and eggs. There's a place downtown called Chang's Kitchen, they do good considering the price.' He burped, covering his mouth, as if expecting something else to come out.

'We can reconsider the idea of food if you want,' I said, surveying his condition.

'Nah, I'll be fine… just the morning blues. Some food will set me straight.'

As Tony lay down with a pillow over his head, battling a secondary wave of nausea, I entered the second compartment of the garage, which was kind of like a cluttered alley full of boxes of junk. In front of me was the automated garage door—seldom used—and to the left was Todd's room. His door was always shut, conveying a greater message to everyone on the outside. I didn't blame him. I had come to understand him and his desire for solitude. His room was his place of peace, once he locked his door, he was momentarily free from life and all its complications.

I knocked two times.

Waited.

'Who is it?' Todd grumbled, his voice raspy and a lot deeper than it normally was.

'Corey,' I replied.

'Enter!'

I did so only to find Todd topless wearing sweatpants, pumping out sets of push-ups. He tilted his head upright in-between reps and said, 'What's the matter, Corey?'

'I was just wondering if you wanted to join me and Tony for breakfast, seeing we got paid last night.'

He halted, frozen in the plank position. 'What do you have in mind?'

'Chang's,' I replied. 'Tony reckons it's the best bang for your buck.'

'Chang's is shit,' Todd muttered. 'But then again, just about every joint in this town is.'

'So, that's a yes?'

He nodded, rising to his feet. 'I'll drive. When do you wanna go?'

'As soon as Tony pulls himself together. He's falling apart back there.'

'That's what vodka, rum, and beer does to you, nothing he doesn't deserve.' Todd threw on his jacket and put on his black beanie.

It was 9.A.M and we just missed the morning rush. The atmosphere at Chang's was carefree with no regard to time, but this would all change come lunch time. I got my bacon and eggs which were cooked to perfection—the bacon crispy, eggs fried nice and quick, running down my plate. Even Tony returned to the land of the living once he replenished his depleted body with protein and caffeine. We scraped our plates clean and leaned back into our chairs, for once happy to have our bellies full.

But the mood all changed when Stretch barged through the door. He had a furious way of walking resembling an urgent gallop. He looked like he was about to pop the moment he spotted us in the corner. His eyes bulged out of his skeletal face, leering at us like our existence pissed him off ridiculously. Eventually he forced a smile that would make a child cry.

'How the hell did you know you'd find us here?' I said.

'Mate,' Stretch began, 'I know ye every move...' He looked pleased with himself, the look of a fool who blew his own trumpet one too many times. I doubted Stretches perceptual abilities, he was the kind of guy who didn't even know the name of the New Zealand prime minister.

'I've got a job for ye,' Stretch said. He pulled up a chair, spinning it around and sat on the opposite end.

'And when did you start calling the shots?' said Todd. 'Typical Stretch, trying to overrun mum's authority again, aye? Thought you'd learn by now. You've already walked this path and where did it lead you?'

Stretch lost all the colour in his face. His eyes glazed over, and then suddenly; he lost all expression marking him as unreadable. 'Look at ya, my boy,' he said, the way a father would to a son. 'You've grown an actual pair of balls since I've been locked up.' He leaned in close to Todd. 'Jus so ya know, they can be ripped off if yur not careful.'

He abruptly arose from his chair and flew at Todd. His right hand bound to his throat, his left gripping Todd's testicles.

Todd released a high-pitched shriek.

Worrisome heads turned on the other tables. Stretch didn't seem to care much for the show he was putting on, he was trying to make a point, if not to Todd, but to every one of us.

'After everythin' I've done for ya, ye got the nerve to

talk to me like that? Ye jus like yur mother! I shoulda left you to starve while ye mum was in rehab.' Stretch got so close to Todd's face a bystander would be convinced he was about to bite him. 'We're all ya got, kid. Turning yur back on me is like turning ya back on yer entire family, remember that! So, are you in or what?'

Todd grunted as Stretch squeezed harder.

'I can't hear ya?'

'Yes,' Todd said breathlessly, 'I'm in.'

'Good,' said Stretch, releasing his vice-grip. He plonked himself back on his seat. 'It's me daughter's birthday, seeing I'm outta jail thought I'd buy 'em somethin' nice. Saw a bike shop on the corner of Pine Ave, I need you boys to do some shoppin' for me.'

'We don't have enough coin between us to buy a bike,' said Tony.

Stretch laughed. 'You don' need no money, boy. Ya jus' need to pedal fast.'

'What will the other two of us do?' I said. 'Flee the scene on foot? We'll be scooped up by the cops in no time.'

'Nup,' said Stretch. 'You'll be riding on two other bikes. Thought I'd get me two other girls bikes as well… you know, as a get outta jail present from their daddy. Shop closes at five. I want 'em by midnight, me mate and I will be driving up the line to drop em off by morning.' Stretch got up to leave. 'And Todd, yur in charge, if ya like ye balls where they are, I wouldn't recommend fucking up.'

The entire cafe seemed to sigh with relief as Stretch

went to leave, but when he was halfway out the door he halted as if he had forgotten something. He rushed back over to us; his maddened little eyes set on Todd.

'Why the fuck you always hidin' behind that beanie!' he shouted. 'You ashamed, boy? Have some fuckin' pride!' He ripped off Todd's beanie, throwing it to the floor and stomped on it like it embodied a philosophy he despised. He fixed his hands to Todd's head, pulling him to his feet. 'See this everyone!' he yelled. 'This kid's a skin-head! Trained by the fuckin Kaos originals! Tell all ye monkey friends, Todd's his name!' He displayed the swastika scar on the back of Todd's neck before throwing him to the floor and rushed out the door to destroy the next sorry bugger who crossed paths with him.

Tony and I helped Todd up. He lowered his head in shame as all the beady eyes from the customers stared at him, petrified and equally repulsed.

'Let's get out of here,' said Todd under his breath.

Just as we went to leave, an Asian man appeared from out of the kitchen. 'Get out of my shop!' he yelled. 'No welcome! No welcome!'

***

Half an hour before midnight we stuck close to the shadows and crept toward the bike shop on Pine Ave. Prior to our midnight plunder, we dropped into the shop to seek out the most age-appropriate bikes and where they resided. Fortunately, an array of pink bikes with sparkling tinsel draped over the ends of the handles were mounted on stands in the shop window. All we had to do was hack our way through the window and pedal around the back end of the block to take a short cut to Todd's house. On the way over Todd found a large enough rock that he wrapped in his jacket and lugged it all the way there.

'Ready?' asked Todd.

We nodded.

The coast was clear. Not a soul in sight.

'Once I smash through the window, kick around the broken glass.' Todd lifted the rock above his head, his knees bent to build as much momentum as possible. He biffed the rock at his target, causing a shattering incision at the centre of the window. Tony and I booted through the glass until we had an entry point. We swooped on in, one after the other.

Wheeling out the bikes we jumped on the awkward little seats, our knees nearly touching the handlebars as we pedalled down the block. It would have been quite a scene to the public eye, three twenty-year-olds pedalling down the street like maniacs, riding pink bikes built for ten-year-old girls.

Stretch and his meth-head mate were waiting for us on the corner of Edgecombe Street. They loaded the bikes into the trunk and blitzed up state highway two, heading straight for the countryside of Hawkes bay without stopping. But what he didn't anticipate was a checkpoint just outside of Waipukarau.

Highway patrol checked Stretch and his buddies ID

and ran them through the system. It turned out Stretch's ex-wife had a restraining order against him and he wasn't permitted to entering the region. The bikes never made it to his kids, who more than likely didn't know their dad existed anywhere other than old boxes of photographs their mother had left to rot in the basement.

Todd never told me the extent of what Stretch did to have a restraining order put against him, but I knew he would have left her hanging over the edge too many times.

Stretch was sentenced to a two-month lock-down back in Upper Hutt so he could be monitored while the court processed his sentencing. He was a repeat offender. A product of conduct disorder, the court concluded. What this meant for us was having to share the garage with him. The court thought he was better left alongside his family for moral support. What a joke. The way I saw it, Stretch was without a family, he had cheated them, used and abused them the way he did to everyone who was unfortunate enough to say they knew him. He was an outcast like the rest of us, but he was *outside the outside*, too far away from himself to even know the self who was trapped inside the body he called Stretch.

Jacklyn made him sleep in the garage alongside us until the court delivered his fate. We helped carry his stuff into the garage—which wasn't much—and stacked it in a pile in the corner. Stretch drew the line of his portion of the garage. I didn't care too much, he only had a few more cobwebs, plus, it was colder on his side, anyway.

'I know every idem, every drop of dust on me stuff,' Stretch barked at us, as he lay a bed sheet over a mattress we retrieved from storage. 'If any of ye touch anythin'... you'd be dead.'

Stretch's life had swooped even lower than it was before—if it was at all possible. If he wasn't already considered a danger to himself—or anyone in that regard, now he was a man who had long accepted he was present in a world where everything he touched turned to ashes.

Day by day, he sat in the corner of the garage, his knees buckled up to his face, glumly drinking whiskey straight from the bottle while chain smoking meth like cigarettes. Tony and I left him alone. It didn't once occur to me to check in to see if he was okay. He was a miserable product of his own decisions. Maybe somewhere in his chemically tainted mind he knew it, but it didn't stop him from indulging in his depression.

Chapter 17

Clark scored us a job a bit closer to home. It would prove to be an easy one. The get together was said to be full of *friendlies* (friends of Jacklyn) so we knew precaution wasn't necessary. Todd wasn't to accompany us; Jacklyn gave him the night off saying he looked like he needed it. After the incident at Chang's Kitchen, something wasn't the same about him. He locked himself in his room not even rising for evening grub or supper. Stretch was pretty harsh on him, I guess. The whole town would be talking about the incident by now and rallying the town-folk, handing out pitchforks and flaming sticks. I felt sorry for Todd. The moment of his birth he was destined to be caught up in a life of corruption. The way I saw it, he never really ever had a say in his own life. Either he followed orders or Stretch taunted him until he'd bend. As for Jacklyn, I saw beyond her stitched up motherly mask. Jacklyn and Stretch were one in the same, though she was just a bit more subtle and covered herself with the idea she was the glue to the family, but anyone with half a brain would see different.

Tony and I were getting ready to head out, each of us took turns in the shower that spewed out nothing but cold water. We came back into the garage to find Stretch sharing a pipe with Charlie. Over the past couple of days, she had treaded around us like we were shards of broken glass, but finally she was beginning to come out of her shell.

Stretch chugged down his second bottle of whiskey, reciting stories over a pipe. Once again, as always, his stories selfishly rolled off his tongue as if he were talking to himself in the mirror. Charlie didn't seem to mind, the more meth she smoked, the more gripping his tales became. She listened eagerly, her wired emerald eyes appearing to be pried open by an invisible force, as she latched onto every syllable, every flicker of sound bursting off his tongue.

Charlie's hood was pulled up over her head, her black hair draped over her shoulders, her make-up gloomy, done up with black lipstick and thick, dark mascara. Stretch carried on with his endless drool he called conversation, as Charlie shifted her bright eyes to me and Tony.

'Corey! Tony!' she exclaimed excitedly. 'Come join us.' She smiled, lighting up the filthy garage for a second, and patted down the concrete floor beside her.

I glanced at Stretch—who, to my surprise, was still blabbering nonsense. He was so consumed by himself he seemed to forget he was having a conversation with

Charlie. The thought of sharing a moment with Stretch repelled me. I'd rather go to church than sit and listen to him.

'We're actually on our way out,' I said.

The lights in her eyes dimmed.

'We'll be back soon, though,' Tony added. 'Just in case this fella bores you to sleep!'

'I don't think I'll be sleeping for the next two days,' she replied, packing the pipe with more crystals.

'I'd mind that stuff, aye,' I said, pointing to the pipe. 'If you smoke too much, you'll start looking like Jacklyn!'

'Ah, ease up, Cor,' said Tony. 'She's old enough to make her own decisions.'

To me she was just a little girl who'd do anything to numb her infinite sadness. But what she did was none of my business. I knew nothing about the road she'd walked, or her tribulations which sparked her need for escape, but what I did know is making a habit of that stuff would only load more burdens on your back.

'We gotta go,' said Tony. 'Don't go crazy.' Tony nodded at Stretch. He was away with the fairies mumbling to himself, nurturing his bottle of whiskey between his legs.

Charlie laughed and put down the pipe—hopefully forever.

'I've got a fridge full of beers,' Tony said to her. 'If you guard them for me and make sure this nutter keeps his greasy claws off them, I'll share them with you when we get back, how's that sound?'

***

We lurked in the driveway for ten minutes. Tony repeatedly checked the time on his phone, then checked his wrist as if he was wearing a watch. 'Where the hell is she? "I'll be ready in twenty minutes" she said, Jeez!'

'This should be short and sweet,' I said. 'We'll be back in no time, then we can chill out with Charlie… I don't know how I feel about leaving her alone with Stretch, though—did you see the state of him?'

'She'll be fine,' said Tony dismissively. He whacked me playfully on the shoulder. 'All we gotta do is hand out these samples, then we're done. Like you said, short and sweet.'

'Yeah,' I muttered. 'But it is Stretch we are talking about here—a wounded Stretch who doesn't give a shit about anything, himself included.'

'But Todd's only a few doors down,' said Tony.

'I guess you're right. It's just lately I've grown to expect the worst.'

Our conversation was interrupted by the back door slamming shut. We were hit in the face with potent perfume and cheap hair spray as the hollow taps of Jacklyn's high heels echoed throughout the driveway.

'You got the goods?' asked Jacklyn. 'It's got to be an ounce exactly between you.'

'We got it,' I said.

We were heading for Todd's car when Amos scrambled after Jacklyn. 'Mommy!' he cried.

'Mommy's gotta go, hun. Todd's in his room, he'll

sort you out some dinner. Mama loves you.' Jacklyn blew kisses and went for the driver's seat. As she reversed, Amos climbed on top of the flattened stone pillar and sat with his thumb in his mouth, where he would remain until his mother returned, completely oblivious to what horrors were about to take place meters away from him.

***

The gathering was like a dope pushers convention full of drug slinging nobodies who existed in the realms of pseudo-names, cash payments, wearing personalities like they were an assortment of clothing on a rack. We did what was expected of us and handed out the samples to dealers who were looking to buy in bulk and left once the deed was done. Jacklyn, however, was in her element, flirting up a storm with sleazebags who wanted only one thing. We decided to not wait for her and left the party on foot, taking as many beers as we could carry.

Back at Jacklyn's we found Amos still perched on top of the flattened stone pillar like a gargoyle statue. He was shivering in his pyjamas with nothing on his feet.

'Come on,' said Tony. 'You wanna see Todd? Jump down I'll take you.'

'No!' Amos exclaimed. 'Mommy!'

'Your mum's not gonna be back for a while,' I said.

He refused to come down but when Tony told him Todd had a heap of toys in his room he reconsidered. Chief howled at us as we stepped through the back gate, startled by our shadows but he eased off once he heard our voice.

I wrapped my hand around the doorknob but for some reason I couldn't bring myself to open it. My stomach dropped and swirled with dreadful butterflies. Something was wrong, but what? Some intuitive alarm sounded in my mind. I couldn't pin down why, but I just knew something was terribly wrong.

'What are you waiting for, dude,' said Tony. 'Those beers in the fridge aren't gonna drink themselves!'

'Shhhh,' I whispered, pressing a finger to my lips. 'Listen…'

Tony hammered his hands to his hips and frowned, then he picked up Amos off the cold grass. 'The kid's an ice cube, bro. We need to get him inside.'

'*Listen*,' I said again, this time urgently.

Tony arched his head closer to the door. We heard all kinds of faint moans and groans. There was a bang followed by another airy cry.

'It sounds like someone's getting it on in there,' said Tony, smirking.

'I don't think so,' I said. 'It sounds like someone's in pain.'

'Well, let's take a look for ourselves,' said Tony, reaching for the doorknob.

He fiddled around with it. It was locked. As he rattled the door the sounds within the garage ceased a little too quickly. There was a deadened silence, the type you'd find at a cemetery past midnight. What we heard next sent chills down my spine. '*Help!*' a muffled voice blurted.

I took a step back and booted the door. It took me

numerous attempts but eventually I got it open. We ran into the garage unsure of what to expect. The first thing I noticed was Stretches jeans were around his ankles. He was on top of a mangled mess of black hair. He bared his teeth and snarled at us. Charlie was lying on her stomach, her tights torn in places, they too were around her ankles, she looked like a helpless fish who washed ashore, unable to move, unable to edge her way toward her freedom that was so close, yet impossibly far.

She was stuck within a residual nightmare where there was not a thing she could do but take it, accept every violent thrust of the hips, every rhythmic stab, every invasive blow, shattering her innocence, the innocence she would no longer relate to as she became a stranger to herself, feeling dirty, like she was the one who had done something wrong and it was nobody's fault accept for her own.

I charged at Stretch tackling him off her. Charlie crawled to the opposite end of the garage appearing battered, her mind in pieces. I noticed blood splattered in-between her thighs. She was too shaken to even pull her tights back up as she gazed despairingly at the man who violated her.

I guarded Charlie as Tony pulled her tights back up and tried to hold her together, meanwhile Amos hugged Tony's knee unsure of what was going on.

'Call the fucking cops!' I shouted at Tony.

'Ya'll do no such thing!' Stretch boomed. 'Dat is if ye wanna live to see another day!'

Through all the commotion Todd barged through the

door, his headphones resting around his neck, his pistol in his hand.

'What's going on!' he demanded.

'He fucking raped her!' Tony shouted, tearing up.

Todd slowly made his way to the centre of the garage and shielded us all. 'You two, get them outta here.' He was surprisingly calm. Focused. Ready for anything.

Tony helped Charlie to her feet and took Amos by the hand, leading them to the kitchen. I stayed put, refusing to leave Todd's side.

'What are you waiting for, Corey!' Todd snapped. 'Get outta here and take care of the others!'

'But Todd—'

'Get out!' he yelled.

I stared at Stretch one last time, taking a mental photograph of a scene that would haunt me for the rest of my life, and left to find the others.

'Big man with a gun, aye?' said stretch, taking a step closer to Todd.

Todd raised his sidearm.

'Don't move another inch!' he demanded. 'I'll blow your fucking face off!'

'You ain't got it in ya,' said Stretch, hardly bothered. 'I had ye balls in my hands jus' the other day. I'll tell ya, boy, they weren't very big… so what makes ye think you'll shoot me?'

'Don't doubt me,' said Todd. 'I'll do whatever it takes to protect this family, and if that means putting a bullet in you… so be it.'

Todd had every reason to put a bullet in Stretch.

Everything Todd had become was because of Stretch. He was a loner because of Stretch, he was afraid to love because of Stretch, he was lost because of Stretch.

Stretch chuckled and cracked a smile, raising his hands mockingly to the ceiling. 'All right, if ye gonna shoot me, shoot me already. Stop wasting time.'

Todd rapidly contemplated his options. Seconds turned to hours.

'I knew it,' said Stretch, laughing it off. 'You ain't got it in ya. I raised a boy with a pussy…'

Todd's hand trembled, his grip tightening around the pistol, his finger twitching around the trigger. He exhaled and lowered his weapon. 'You're right,' said Todd, 'I can't kill you—I won't.'

Stretch folded his arms and grinned.

'I'd rather watch you rot in prison while you cross days off calendars, counting down what's left of your life, until you're sentenced to another kind of prison, hell…'

Chapter 18

Chaos was all around me. Tony screamed and shouted threats toward the garage, but in no time his screams were drowned out by police sirens. Convulsive blue and red lights tore through the curtains, my vision, my racing thoughts, and finally causing tears in my own eyes. Amos whined alongside the sirens, hiding his face in Tony's denim jacket, dizzied by the whirlwind of emotions his innocent mind couldn't grapple. Charlie remained silent on the couch, her eyes dilated and distant. She looked like she was trapped within a never-ending nightmare, praying to wake up and for this to all be over. But this was her reality, an unfortunate chain of events somehow we all played part in.

I made Charlie a cup of tea and sat her down at the kitchen table. My foster mother use to make me a cup of tea during times of distress as a child, so I thought it was worth a try. But Charlie needed a little more than a cup of tea to make this all go away. She held the cup close to her trembling lips, blowing tenderly into it.

'Everything is going to be okay,' I said, rubbing her back.

A dam of emotions broke, and so the tears fell. 'It's never okay,' she sobbed. 'I don't understand why these bad things always happen to me… aren't they supposed to happen to bad people? I'm a good person. Yeah, I've fucked up in the past, but I don't deserve this!'

I pulled her close and thought, only in this world would someone exploit someone's kindness. Only in this world would someone rape a young girl who was in the process of developing their character.

'I can't shut my eyes without seeing his face… all I see is him, all I feel is the weight of his body on top of mine…' she shuddered. 'And the smell of alcohol on his breath… it makes me sick.'

Charlie delved into her subconscious, unearthing what she buried in the darkest corners of the mind. But no matter how hard she suppressed the past it would always be there to dictate her every move, it would always be there to wage war on her when she encountered any future ties of intimacy.

I saw beyond the walls she had built around her. I wish I could have shown her what I saw, what I felt, otherwise there's no way she'd believe me. I saw a girl bursting with life, a healer who was able to attune themselves to the broken and help them repair their lives. Her only want and only need was to serve the people. But Charlie was never given a chance to mend herself. She was like a beacon of light amidst a cloud of swarming demons. They pounced on her, they smothered her, they violated her, sucking the light out of her until she became just as empty, just as soulless as they were.

'Charlie,' I repeated, trying to bring her feet back to the ground. 'Everything is going to be okay.'

She stared through me without blinking, black gunky mascara dribbled down her cheeks. She was too far gone. What was left of her sanity had been squeezed out in less than a few minutes.

An officer knocked on the front door and told us he was coming in. As the cop took a statement from Charlie, we watched the other policemen march Stretch down the driveway with his hands cuffed behind his back. Todd followed close behind him, also in cuffs.

As I'd later discover, Stretch ratted Todd out about his unregistered pistol. Stretch knew he was going down, so he wanted everyone to go down with him. On the flip side, the police only kept Todd in interrogation for a few hours. He simply told the officer the gun was not his and how Stretch was trying to wipe his dirt on someone else's hands in attempt to reduce his inevitable sentencing. The cops lapped it up, they took any excuse to lock Stretch up for good.

After a thumb twiddling two hours a police car dropped Todd home. He burst through the back door and frantically searched the house. 'Where is he?' said Todd.

'Who?' I asked.

'Amos for god sake!'

'Relax,' said Tony. 'He's on the couch fast asleep.'

He ran into the lounge where he found Amos wrapped up in Tony's denim jacket, peacefully sleeping with his thumb in his mouth while cartoons played on the TV.

Todd sighed, holding his hand over his heart, and retraced his steps back to the kitchen, taking a seat beside Charlie. 'What a night,' he said, shaking his head. Tony popped the top off a beer and placed it in front of him. Todd took a long swig, fixing his eyes to Charlie. 'He's gone. You don't have to worry about ever seeing him again.'

She dried her eyes with a tissue and hugged herself, peering out the window and into the night. We then heard approaching footsteps and drunken murmurs. The back door swung open. Jacklyn tripped over her own foot, hanging loosely off some bloke's shoulder who looked to be a bit older than us, giggling like she was seventeen all over again.

'Where's Amos?' she slurred. 'Is my baby, okay?'

'He's sleeping,' said Todd. 'You know you left him outside with nothing on his feet for most of the night.'

'I told him to go find you,' Jacklyn said defensively.

'Well, maybe next time you can communicate with me instead of a toddler who is still learning how to talk!' Todd turned to the guy who Jacklyn had brought home with her. 'Who's this?'

'This is—' she seemed to forget his name.

'Aaron,' the guy said, holding out his hand.

'Don't bother,' said Todd. 'Come morning you'll be a nobody once she's done with you.'

190

Aaron looked slightly offended, he backed off, raising an eyebrow at Jacklyn.

'Where's Stretch?' Jacklyn asked.

We glanced at each other. Nobody wanted to answer her question.

'Wait a second!' she shouted. 'What the hell are you boys doing in my kitchen!' She then softened her voice as she spoke to Charlie. 'Charlie, hun, you're fine—' her tone turned nasty again '—but these boys aren't supposed to be in here!'

'Stretch raped her,' said Todd.

'What?' said Jacklyn.

'I should go,' said Aaron, taking a step toward the back door.

'No, Aaron—stay. You've been drinking, there's plenty of room in my bed—'

'I'll call a cab,' he said. He smiled awkwardly at us and slipped out the door, realizing for once in the twenty-five years he had served on the earth sex wasn't worth it.

'I beg your pardon, Todd. Is this some kind of fucked up joke!' said Jacklyn angrily.

Charlie burst into tears.

'I wish it was,' Todd replied.

Chapter 19

Jacklyn was out for a few days sourcing MDMA for Tony and me to distribute the following weekend. But I knew she was trying to distance herself from Charlie, so she didn't have to deal with the mess her brother had left behind.

Tony and I looked forward to making enough money so we too could distance ourselves from this melting pot. After maybe two more MDMA deals we agreed we were done. After the ordeal with Stretch, we decided there was no place for us here. We'd hand in our resignation—if that was at all applicable—and flee south to Golden Bay where the sun shone twice as hard in the summer. Me and Tony had never been down south before, it seemed like our best option for a much-needed retreat, and even better, no one knew our names or faces.

We took advantage of Jacklyn's absence and sought refuge beside the fireplace looking after Charlie. She stayed in bed for the remainder of the weekend, where she found her temporary escape within movies and getting high.

I suggested she see a counsellor, but she wanted no part in it. She explained to me how she went through the system as a kid. I imagined being just another tick in the box, stuck in a brightly coloured room with motivational quotes on the walls, sitting on chairs that were ever so slightly facing away from each other, as some fresh-faced graduate who was out to save the world tried to level with you. The thought alone made me want to bash my head on one of those motivational quotes on the wall.

'You've got to talk to someone,' I said. 'Charlie, I know it's hard, but you can't shut the door on this and live your life like nothing ever happened. It won't get any easier, something like this doesn't go away on its own.'

She grabbed the last handful of chips and carelessly dropped the empty packet to the floor, wiping her sticky fingers on Jacklyn's sheets. 'There's nobody out there who can help me,' she said. 'And you're definitely not one of them, so quit trying, okay!'

'I'm not giving up on you—and Tony sure as hell isn't giving up on you. Todd for Christ-sake went completely out of his way to help you, and Jacklyn—'

'Jacklyn's using me for child support payments.'

'I don't care about Jacklyn, the point I'm trying to make is *we* care about you.'

'But you hardly know me.'

'Charlie, you need to let us help you.'

She sat up in the bed, sighing. 'Look, I can't see a counsellor, it won't do me any good. When I was little

Child Youth and Family took me off my mum, she loved drugs more than she loved me. So they put me in a home with heaps of other kids. I never went hungry, but there were too many of us to take care of, the loud ones always got all the attention—and the quiet ones, like me, either came in last or were forgotten completely.' She paused and took a deep breath. 'They used to gang up on me...'

'Who did?'

'The others... I kept to myself, but they were all really *out there* kind of people. At that age, people tend to not be very accepting of other people's differences. They used to beat me up. They teased me. They took my share of the food, and the other girls used to...'

'What did they do to you?'

'They used to touch me at night in the girls dorm, and put things inside of me while they pointed and laughed... I was stuck there for two years—two years of abuse!'

'Why didn't you tell anyone?'

'I couldn't,' she snapped. 'If I did, they'd find out, they said they'd kill me—not that anyone cared about me there, anyway... So, I did the only thing I knew, run away. The streets became my home, a dangerous place for a teenage girl. If it wasn't for Homeless Harry, I would have been anyone's for the taking.'

'You know Homeless Harry!'

She smiled and nodded. 'He taught me how to read, he taught me his street philosophies and most importantly he taught me how to love myself.' She rolled up her shirt sleeve, revealing razor blade scars scaling all

194

the way down her arms.

I shook my head in disbelief. 'I knew Harry, he was a friend of mine. Did you meet him out in the city?'

'Nah, met him at a soup kitchen in Johnsonville.'

'He does have a way of getting around,' I said. 'Small world, ain't it?'

'Yeah,' she muttered.

'So you must be familiar with his Wellington City Blues?'

Her eyes lit up and she nodded. 'We are the embodiments of his song.'

'What do you mean?'

'You, me, Tony, Todd, Jacklyn—even Stretch, we are the sombre sounds of the town... the blues of Wellington city.'

I meditated on her words, but it wasn't until later on I understood what she meant. I offered her a cigarette and lit it for her.

'To me,' she continued, 'Miranda is dead, not even a thing of the past, it's like she never existed. That is until I became Charlie. For me it was like rebirth. A clean slate in life. But the pain of yesterday sticks with me no matter how hard I try to forget. But now I have a new wound, wanna see it? I didn't want to do it, but I have a bad habit of hurting myself. Now Stretch has become a part of me forever...' She rolled up her other sleeve. On her wrist was a gnarly gash, fresh and still bleeding.

'Jesus, I'll get you a bandage.'

'No need to,' she said. 'I like the feeling.'

I came back with a bandage, anyway, insisting she put

it on.

'So what are you going to do next?' I asked as I wrapped up her wrist.

'I'm probably gonna put on another movie, why?'

'No, I mean… what's your next move in life, you can't stay at Jacklyn's forever.'

'I'm not sure. There aren't too many other places to go. I'm just gonna stay here until I figure everything out. And you?'

'I'm on the same boat,' I replied. 'I've got ideas, but they'll remain ideas until we're successful with our next job, so I'm not sure… but what I do know is I can't stay here for too long.'

She nodded in silent agreement and said, 'Wanna watch something with me?'

Chapter 20

As the weekend rolled over, me and Tony were called to Clark's office, our long-anticipated job had finally arrived. It was to be the one that would end it all, so we hoped. Clark was perched on his leather chair dressed in a maroon hoodie with matching track-pants that looked like his mother had bought them for him.

'Hey dudes,' he said in his congested voice. 'I got a big one for you this Friday, you available—yeah you're available—this one's going down homies!' He formed a gang symbol with his hand. 'You don't wanna miss it. Now's the time to make some *G's!*

'What makes this job so special?' asked Tony.

'Bros, I'll show you...' He dramatically pressed the space bar on his keyboard. On his screen Google Maps appeared. A red flag highlighted the destination, using his mouse he zoomed in as Lower Hutt came into sight.

'I still don't get it,' said Tony.

'Let me break it down for you, bra,' said Clark. 'Rich

kids don't have a taste for bushy weed. Rich kids like expensive things, like *smack-bang* ecstasy pills! I can only assume their parents have vacated to their beach house for a week, so these guys will want to party until the sun comes up. They'll buy you both out. The party is scheduled for Friday, it's a once in a lifetime opportunity to make some big bucks! Just tell them it's specially formulated stuff imported from the UK, guaranteed to knock their socks off. Remember, this isn't some trashy garage party, I need you two to be showered, shaved, and dressed in clean clothes come Friday. For this to be a success you need to act civilized, you know, *sophisticated*. Todd's your ride and security for the evening, so I'd imagine you won't run into any trouble—as long as you don't harass any of their girls… that goes for you, Tony.'

'Yeah, yeah,' muttered Tony. 'Just so you know, last time those girls chased me, it's not always the boys who do the chasing. But you'd know all about that, wouldn't you, Clark?'

***

Friday came about like a heavy gust of wind storming through a clouded sky. We waited for Jacklyn in the kitchen (on dealing days we were allowed in the house), she returned with the pills divided into tiny snap-lock bags stuffed within a brown paper bag. Handing the drugs to Tony she said, 'Be wise, use this,' she gestured to her head, 'you're now carrying a ticking time-bomb. Do not draw any unwanted attention to yourself and stay in

Todd's line of sight. Even though these are rich pricks we are dealing with, it isn't gonna stop them from trying to jump you.' Her motherly tone was drowned out by her business-like facade. 'I've counted how many pills you're holding, and I've calculated how much money I expect you to return with. So don't go trying to play me as a fool, all right.' She pointed a stiff finger at us, refusing to break eye-contact until she knew we received her message.

'Yes, mam,' we said.

'Good luck and I'll see you later,' she said, fading down the hall to Clark's office.

I waited until her footsteps became faint and crept in the direction of Jacklyn's bedroom.

'What the hell are you doing?' said Tony. 'She'll kill you if she catches you in there.'

I raised a finger to my lips and whispered, 'Meet you in the car.'

I tapped on the door.

'Who is it?' said Charlie.

I slipped into the bedroom. She was still in bed. The curtains were drawn, and the blankets were pulled up to her face as a movie played in the background. She was without make-up which made her look her actual age.

'I'm just checking up on you,' I said. 'It's a bit harder with Jacklyn back home. Is she looking after you?'

'Yeah,' she replied. 'She's been giving me weed and MDMA as if it were anti-depressants.'

I shook my head. 'That's only going to make things worse.'

'After the second come-down I decided to stop taking them—I can't stand ecstasy come downs... are you guys on your way out?'

I nodded. 'Wish us luck. Anyway, I better go, I just wanted to see how you were doing.'

I turned to leave.

'Corey!' Charlie called out. 'Be careful out there.'

***

The houses along the Hutt Valley boulevard were all two story—some three— with double garages, some houses had five cars parked in the driveway. *One for each member of the family*, I thought.

The engine choked as Todd steered his rust-bucket car down another street. If a cop saw us in this part of town, we would probably be pulled over immediately. The houses seemed to demand respect from the rickety homes in the slums only a couple of suburbs down. On this side of the valley, it was easy to forget about scumbags and hoodlums, dealers and people like Stretch, yet they were right in the middle of the chaos, protected by an imaginary bubble made of income and luxurious cars.

Following the address Clark had given us, we cruised past each house, keeping our eyes on letterbox numbers. We came to a dead end of the street with nowhere to park. The street was cluttered with vehicles belonging to the party guests.

'This is as close as I can get,' said Todd. He cursed

the enormous fence blocking his view into the party. 'Bastards,' he mumbled, 'I'm gonna have to go commando behind a hedge for the night—even then, I'll struggle to keep eyes on you.'

'We'll make it quick,' I said nervously.

'No,' Todd said. 'Don't leave until you've made your money worth.'

'What are we waiting for?' said Tony. 'Every second we waste we are losing money for our ferry ticket.'

We entered the brightly lit driveway speckled with sphere shaped solar lights guiding us to the front door. Surrounding us was a tall concrete fence with spear tipped finishings, there was absolutely no way to jump over without having to get stitches, Todd would have to take a risk and make a bolt through the driveway.

We bypassed the front door and followed a pebble path through a well nurtured garden, walking for what felt like ten minutes until finally we arrived in the backyard. The music was no longer a distant murmur and we were able to make out lyrics. In order to get to the heart of the party we had to climb wooden stairs leading to an outdoor deck on the second floor. There was no other point of entry. This minimized our chances of gaining pack approval. We had to truly appeal to them in the first ten seconds of contact, otherwise we'd be run out of town by a clan of rich kids.

'We're gonna have to wing it,' I said. 'How does a stranger rock up to someone's party and blend in anyway?'

'They just do it,' said Tony. 'They think on their feet,

they know the right thing to say at the right time.'

Tony and I grabbed two beer bottles from out of the recycling bin, holding them close to our chest so we looked like a ten-o-clock drunk, and made our way up the stairs. A bunch of guys and girls who looked to be in their twenties were sprawled out in the spa pool, drinking beer and bobbing their heads to music. Others were scattered over the deck in small circles smoking pot, doing the old *puff puff pass.*

'Who's that?' said a girl in the spa.

'Eh, what's your names?' one guy demanded from the pot smoking circle.

'I haven't seen your faces around here,' said another.

'I'm calling the cops!' One skittish girl uttered in the background.

Amidst all the commotion a guy with blond hair and blue eyes exited the sliding glass door and walked towards us. He seemed to shine, glisten like he was brand new. He was clean shaven and had a confident way of walking, as if everything always worked in his favour, and failure and wrong doings were a world away. As he approached us, I heard people nearby say, 'Connor, you know these guys?' He ignored them, squinting at us as he drew closer.

'Corey Gnosis? Tony McKnight? Someone pinch me cos I must be dreaming… I haven't seen you guys since Mr Hanes year 10 maths class!'

My jaw dropped.

Tony shook a little, rubbing his eyes.

'You do remember me, don't you?' he asked. 'Connor

Daraleah. Aberdeen College. Graduated 2018—but you two wouldn't know, you were well gone by then.' He grinned, his teeth a pearly white. On the surface, there was nothing wrong with him. He was handsome, charming, athletic, intelligent… but one had to go digging to find the *real* Connor Daraleah, the Connor Daraleah both Tony and I knew and remembered.

From what I can recall, Connor couldn't fail at anything even if he tried. During our first year of college—the most awkward phase of our lives—he still managed to have four times the number of friends I ever had. Everything he said and did echoed elegance, precision, and the epitome of slickness. But Connor had won too many times in life, so many he didn't know how to lose. I lost too much in my life, and can vouch for Tony, too. We were losers, but we knew how to lose, when we did win it was a call for celebration. As for Connor, he considered a grade below 80% an utter failure. Coming in 2nd on the 100-meter sprint was just as bad as coming in last. When he didn't get his way, he became a spoiled brat, and would take it out on the ones he thought were beneath him. He was a bully, and he was that much of a chump he'd never admit it.

Connor's buddies staggered out onto the deck to see what all the noise was about. One of them put a brotherly arm over his shoulder and whispered into his ear, but loud enough for us to hear, 'Who's the freaks?'

I immediately recognized him. It was Liam, Connors right hand man, *side-kick* as most called him, or *bitch-boy* as we knew him. He had the same hair style as Connor, combed back like a wavy tunnel of hair, but unlike Connor his hair was brown, his eyes dark. He wore almost identical clothing to him as if he secretly took note of where he shopped—or otherwise Connor, himself, had told him where to shop and where to get his hair cut.

On the other side of Connor was Brett, known to the Dooleys as Shag (they liked to create nicknames based upon peoples appearances). Shag had a mop of frizzy brown hair, he was built for the rugby field and had these broad shoulders that looked like he was hiding padding under his shirt.

'Well spank my ass and call me Corey!' said Shag. 'And who do we have here? No doubt its Corey's butt buddy, Tony the lanky ranga—you still jacking off over that picture of your mum you used as a book marker? Man, I gotta say, she had some nice tits!'

Tony thrust himself forward toward Shag. Connor came between them, waving him off saying, 'He's only kidding—you know, this reunion is bringing back the past, the good and the bad.'

'Whatever,' muttered Tony.

Once I calmed him down it hit me, we were now in the heart of the Dooleys nest. The Dooleys were the patriots of the school. They were the high achievers, the athletes, often clean cut and wore their uniforms correctly, they had an etiquette to follow just like we did, but our etiquettes were on different ends of the spectrum. Most of the Dooleys came from the wealthy side of Lower Hutt, stemming from a long line of picture-perfect families. They were like a pack of holy dogs running freely on Saint Aberdeen's famous fields chasing after a rugby ball. They were praised and looked after, as long as they fulfilled the roles which were expected of them. So the pack of holy dogs sat before their masters, wiggling their tails eagerly, they did their trick, and awaited their treat.

Just as I managed to calm down Tony and I too, was beginning to relax, Liam couldn't help but have the last word. 'Hey Ruby, grab the fire extinguisher from the kitchen!' he said. 'There's a fire on that dudes head!' He approached Tony and jabbed him in the arm. 'Ah, just kidding, bro. Just one for old time sake.'

'Good to see you too, Liam,' said Tony through his teeth, clenching his fist as if it were about to soar right into his throat.

'Liam,' said Connor, 'there's no need to be a dick, we have grown up since those days, isn't that right, Corey?' He smiled at me, his eyes not matching the warmth of his smile. 'Don't look so tense, boys. Join us for a drink. But you gotta tell me, how the hell did you know where I live?'

'Ah, you know,' said Tony, 'we just kept a look out for the most expensive looking house in the Hutt Valley.'

Connor laughed awkwardly. 'You always were the class clown, Tony.'

We followed him over to a circular picnic table with an umbrella pinned up. Connor summoned his girl, Ruby, who manifested like a genie. She had these long, dark Bambi eyelashes glued onto her eyelids that flapped like insect wings every time she blinked. Her lips bright pink and permanently puckered like a blown-up balloon—botox I assumed.

'Babe, could you get us some drinks,' said Connor.

'Of course,' she replied, as if she had carried out this action hundreds of times before.

Connor turned to us. 'What do you fellas want? The bar is filled with every drop of alcohol known to man.'

'Rum and coke,' I said quickly.

'Same here,' said Tony, unable to take his eyes off Liam and Shag.

'Brilliant choice,' said Connor, 'I bought the bottle last summer when I was in Barbados, our hotel was on the coast of Saint Martins.'

He may as well be speaking into the wind, I thought. The way he added in the details of his trip seemed like he said it for himself.

With a smug look on his face, Connor gazed at Ruby. 'You know how I like my rum,' he said.

'I'll take it how he has it,' said Liam.

'Likewise,' said Shag.

She smiled faintly and left to get our drinks. Connor watched her slender hips sway from side to side as she slipped through the veranda door and into the golden lit lounge.

'So,' Connor began, 'I haven't heard much talk about *you*, Tony. But I've heard plenty of rumours—or more so sightings going around about you, Corey.'

'What do you mean?' I said hesitantly.

'What I mean is I've heard people say they've seen

you out in town picking around rubbish bins and squatting in alleys. Tell me, I've got to know, are the rumours true?'

'You don't have to answer him,' said Tony butting in.

'It's okay,' I said to Tony. 'Yes, the rumours are true. But that life is now behind me.'

Liam and Shag couldn't hold back their laughter and exploded in coughing fits. Connor cracked a smile but was better to disguise his amusement. Ruby returned with our drinks and Connor snatched his off the tray. 'For your sake I hope that's true,' he said. 'What are you doing with yourself now?'

I hesitated once more, not knowing how to explain my present situation. Without beating around the bush Tony said, 'We're trying to sell these.' He dropped the brown bag of pills on the tabletop.

The boy's eyes widened.

'A hundred bucks a pop, guaranteed to knock your polo-shirts off,' said Tony.

'One hundred?' Liam blurted. 'I can get them for thirty a pill.'

'What's so special about them?' asked Connor, leaning over the table to get a better look.

'There's remnants of a baboons ass crack in each pill—they're just good, okay,' said Tony. 'Do you want to buy some or not? If not, we can try our luck at the next Richie Rich's party.'

Connor fished out his wallet, throwing two fifty-dollar bills on the table. 'We'll take one, there's too many duds circulating around town at the moment, and my gut tells me your stuff is cut. So we'll sample one and get back to you.'

Tony flicked a small baggie containing one pink pill across the table. Connor plucked the pill out of the bag and held it in-between his index finger and thumb. He looked closely at the pill before placing it on his tongue. 'Hey babe!' he called out to Ruby.

She hurried over.

He poked out his tongue, showcasing the pill to her. She seemed to know what would happen next and leaned in to kiss him. He clasped his hand around her butt, savagely squeezing it like it were a big ball of dough, as their kissing went from intimate to lustful. Eventually she pulled away from him and poked out her tongue, revealing the pink pill now resting on hers. She reached for her glass of white wine and washed it down.

Chapter 21

It was the longest hour of my life, sort of like baring an awkward silence with a group of strangers as you scrape for small talk. I had nothing good to say to these people, so I set Connor off, asking questions about the Caribbean in which he didn't hesitate to answer. I listened half-heartedly, zoning out to appoint my attention to Ruby, searching for fireworks going off in her eyes. She just sat there fidgeting with the pearl ring on her finger, looking nervous as to what was going to happen next. Forty-five minutes had passed. Any moment she would be chewing her tongue to pieces.

Every so often I tuned back into Connors conversation, hearing broken ended sentences. '...the heat, you think you know what... like a blanket of hot steam thrown over you...'

I chugged down more rum and blankly stared at Connor, nodding my head.

'... Corey, are you listening to me?' asked Connor.

He shot a hurried glance at his Rolex. 'Nothing's happening and it's been an hour.' He glared at Ruby. 'Babe, how you feeling over there?'

'Fine, my hearts a little racey, and I feel a little nervous, but asides from that, nothing.'

I heard plenty of dissatisfied sighs coming from Liam and Shags direction.

'Well, there you go,' said Connor. 'I thought they were duds. Give me my money back.'

'Give it a few more minutes,' I protested.

'I'm afraid we've given you a moment too long,' replied Connor. 'Look, I've been overly accommodating toward you lads, considering we were never really that close at school. So, do the noble thing and give me my money back and get off my property.'

I slapped his money on the table and stepped to my feet.

'Me and the boys will escort you out, seeing you don't get lost in the garden,' he said.

Tony and I followed them through the pebble-stone path and finally to the enormous concrete fence. We were on our way out when the ten-foot gate began to close on us.

'What's going on?' asked Tony. 'I thought you wanted us to leave!'

'Yeah, I know what you're saying,' said Connor, 'but that's a half-truth. Seeing that you guys just randomly happened to show up, it reminded me of some unfinished business between us.'

'Unfinished business?' I asked.

He nodded. 'Now, your memories might be a little hazy, but I remember being robbed back in 4th form. Does Mr Steele's second period gym class ring any bells for you?'

I hadn't forgotten despite dancing around his question like a thief who had been called out. Back at Aberdeen college word went around about how Shag and his crew were selling cigarettes. Their pride got the best of them, I guess it was edgy and taboo to be selling cigarettes in a place like Aberdeen. Shag let it slip to one too many people and so the game of Chinese whispers began, eventually being passed onto me and Tony during Religious Education. We were the only ones who were bold and stupid enough to take a chance with this information. These guys had it all. We had nothing. At the time it seemed like a plausible excuse to be a thief.

Connor, Shag, and Liam practically had all the same classes together, so when I heard about it during first period, I knew it was our moment to strike. The Dooleys were all packed into 10BD—the smart class—so I knew they had gym second period. Me and Tony instructed our mate from the year below, Mike, to hide around the side of the gymnasium and wait for them to begin their track running warm up. Since Mike was the smallest and the least suspecting of the group, he could pass them by like a gentle breeze. His orders were simple, sneak into the changing room and loot Shags bag.

'You know what I'm talking about, Corey,' said Connor, studying my eyes.

'Stop bullshitting us!' said Liam. 'We know you guys

set it up, we were tipped off. You're just lucky the principle was selecting the junior prefects at the time, otherwise we would have given it to you good!'

'Hand over the pills,' said Connor.

'Like they amount to the same cost!' said Tony.

'With the price of cigarettes nowadays, I'd say the net worth would be pretty close,' Connor said quickly.

'But you said it yourself, they're duds,' I said.

'Every reason to take them off your hands—wouldn't be losing much, would you?'

'Fuck you and your rhetorical questions!' said Tony. 'No deal. They aren't even ours. So what? We stole like twenty packs of smokes from you when we were fifteen years old, big deal. Let's be real, you could buy the same amount right now and it wouldn't put a dent in your bank account… doesn't it satisfy you enough to see what we've become? Exactly what you fuck-wits predicted back when we were kids, drop outs, drug pushers, low life scum. You know what? Fuck you guys, I don't give a shit anymore, take my half.' Teary eyed, Tony turned to me. 'I'll take the blame—I'm over this, Corey. Being around these guys and a place like this is making me sick.' Tony threw his bag of pills at Connors feet.

We stood there a while in a contemplative daze. Shag and Liam looked like they were debating whether they should pulverize our face for old time sake, but then a blood curdling scream echoing from the balcony stole their attention.

'Help! Somebody!' a girl shouted. She repeated herself, each time her voice crackling with escalating urgency.

The guys jogged in the direction of the screams. I trailed behind them, scurrying over the pebble-stone path until I could identify the source of the screams.

'What are you doing?' said Tony, chasing after me. 'Let's bounce—now that we can!'

Ignoring him, I climbed up the stairs and approached a swarm of concerned faces who stood over a girl in a circle. I pushed past guys in short-sleeved button up shirts and young girls in flimsy cocktail dresses to get a better look. It was Ruby, sprawled out on the deck as her entire body shook involuntarily. She lay in a pool of her own vomit, foaming out the side of her mouth, her tongue quivering like a mystified serpent.

'Put her in the recovery position!' someone in the crowd shouted.

She shook so violently one would be convinced a raging earthquake rattled through her bones. The madness seemed to go on forever. Then suddenly, her convulsing body stiffened like a corpse, her wild eyes now absent, fixed to the stars above. An eerie silence swallowed us all.

'She's got no pulse!' I heard a girl kneeling beside her say.

Tony's eyes went innocent. His skin pale.

'Tony, let's go!' I prompted.

He didn't budge. Frozen into shock, trauma, guilt— all the uncanny emotions swirled through him in which death could only invoke.

I tugged on his arm and practically dragged him out

to the street. Immediately I regretted following the Dooley's back to the party. I should have listened to Tony, that way, all of this wouldn't have rested on my conscience—our conscience. We would be blissfully ignorant, unscathed, but now there was no future, no present, only the past flashed through us of a night that would haunt us forever.

Todd was parked on the other side of the street. He blinked his lights at us as we ran over. 'Get us outta here!' I said hurriedly, expecting to hear booming sirens.

'Jesus, settle down,' said Todd casually, completely unaware of the destruction we left behind. He idled the car onto the main road and put his foot down as we powered past the golden fortresses, seeping through the cracks in the Hutt Valley roads as we began our descent into familiar territory.

'Are you going to tell me what the hell is going on?' asked Todd, inspecting the state of Tony through the rear-view.

'I can't tell you—at least not now,' I said, glancing at Tony. He was painfully silent and looked like he was on the brink of tipping into a sea of sadness. As soon as we pulled into the driveway Tony belted for the garage without saying a word.

'Are you gonna tell me what happened?' asked Todd.

'Where the fuck were you?' I said. 'The night was a disaster, from start to finish—we're a whole bag of MDMA down, with no money to vouch for us and we...' I swallowed my tongue. 'We killed a girl.'

'What?' said Todd.

'Tony gave her the pill and she... she just slowly faded away.'

Chapter 22

Tony was sitting in the same corner of the garage where Stretch mournfully smoked his pipe before he was arrested. He was wrapped in his torn sleeping bag, chain smoking and drinking beer. I was surprised to see Charlie out of Jacklyn's bed sitting beside him with her arm around his shoulder as he cried.

Jacklyn's place was a home for disaster. We were all broken in some way or another. Broken people who needed refuge. I'd take Tony and Charlie with me, and Todd as well, I thought. We could retreat to the sombre streets of Wellington city for all I cared, it was safer there than it was here.

I watched on feeling completely powerless, unable to ease my friends suffering. I too, suffered. But I stuffed my guilt in a place in my mind where I knew I'd struggle to find it and focused my attention on our escape to the South Island.

'Can I stay with you guys?' asked Charlie. 'After the

thing with Stretch, Jacklyn's been real funny around me. She's acting like it's my fault that Stretch is back in prison... I'm the victim here, but she's making me feel like I caused this all.'

'You can have my mattress,' I said. 'I'll sleep on the floor.'

'You really don't have to,' she said.

'No, its fine,' I said. 'I'm not going to get much sleep tonight anyway.'

'Thanks, Corey.' She stood up to give me a hug. 'I don't know how I'd deal with this without you guys.'

Tony dried his eyes with the edges of his sleeping bag and took a mighty swig of beer. Charlie lit two cigarettes and handed one to him.

'She would have had a family who loved her, dreams and hope...' Tony began. 'And I took that away from her. I can't forgive myself for what I've done, not this time. My entire life was doomed from the start. Everything is my fault. If I had been a little stronger, I could have got another job and this would have never happened, but I was just so angry at the world I no longer wanted to be a part of it. From the very start life dealt me a shit hand, a hand I could have worked with if I was a stronger person, but I cheated, and it cost someone their life...'

'You are strong, bro,' I said. 'You wouldn't have made it this far if you weren't. The Dooley's would crumble into pieces if they saw everything you've seen, felt everything you feel.'

'I want my mum—I *need* my mum. I want her to hold

me in her arms, like the way she used to when I was a boy. But I can't even have that.' He pulled out the photograph of his mother from his pocket, attempting to draw her spirit close to him. 'If I never existed everything would be okay. Joanna would never have been beaten by her dad, Charlie wouldn't have been raped, and Ruby wouldn't have OD'd... all I ever do is make people suffer.' He turned to me. 'We should never have sat next to each other in Mr. Boyce's class, then none of this would have happened. I'm an outsider—we're outsiders, who are better off dead.'

'We found each other so we could get through this moment,' I said. 'I believe it was Gods will.'

'Was it Gods will that my mother died so young, Corey?' he snarled. 'Was it Gods will that Charlie was raped? That Ruby fucking OD'd?'

To this I said nothing. After an uncomfortable silence I said, 'First thing tomorrow we'll get a ferry to the South Island—we can start a new life and put all of this behind us.'

'It's too late. What's done is done. We have to carry the weight of yesterday,' he said hollowly.

'The past shapes today and what we do today will create a tomorrow, we can change this.'

'No, we can't. It's too late for that.'

On this long and dreary night Tony closed the door on me. He gave up on life and closed his heart off from love. His angels wept over his shoulder, although their healing tears weren't enough to see him through another day. He refused to eat or talk, the only thing he did was drink to make him forget. But he never did. He couldn't even achieve the one thing he desired, for the memories would always resurface once he dropped from the clouds and splattered on the pavement, like a skydiver whose parachute had failed him.

I didn't know how to help him. How can you help someone who cannot help them self? He became dense and stony, a burden to be around. I hated to admit it, but I needed time away from him to gather my own thoughts, my own wellbeing. Selfish, I know. But we can't carry people to the place within them self where healing takes place, only they can. I could guide him, but Tony only listened to the voice of his own suffering.

Days later I decided to take a walk to clear my head. I walked through the park as the sun set behind the hills and reflected on the last thing Tony had said to me before I left. *What will I become beyond this flesh? An eternal lens gazing out the window of the universe? Or would there be nothing to feel… nothing to be?*

I decided enough was enough, come tomorrow I'd get up early and drag him to the ferry terminal. We'd leave without a note or the slightest clue to where we were going. I didn't care where we ended up, I didn't care that we didn't have much money, all that mattered to me was getting him out of Jacklyn's garage.

There are dire consequences that accompany the disconnection from the self. Without it we lose morality, self-respect, and in turn respect for others. The abundance of paths life offers us begins to thin out, choice turns to desperation, and through desperation comes a way out, a means to ease suffering. However freeing themselves from despair, but leaving it behind for others to deal with.

When I arrived back at Jacklyn's I found Todd standing outside the garage as he watched Chief scratch and paw at the door.

'What's up with him?' I asked.

Todd shrugged. 'He's been doing this for the past half hour.' He grabbed Chief by his collar and tried to pull him away from the door.

Chief refused. He pawed on the door and cried some more, making eye contact every so often as if he wanted to be let inside.

'It sounds like he's... nah, that's just silly...'

'Tell me?' I asked.

'Call me crazy, but it sounds like he's mourning... ah I don't know.'

Todd opened the door and Chief bolted through the garage. Todd and I followed behind him. Chief headed straight for where Tony and I slept and started to bark erratically.

Soon we discovered why Chief was so distressed. We found Tony hanging out by himself. He was lifted high off the ground, higher than I've ever seen him before. He was still, silent, which was alarming considering he was always on edge, unable to stand still for a second. His hazel brown eyes were icy as if they were caught in a still frame. His face pale and washed of emotion. He was blank. There was no desire in his eyes. No intent. He seemed to be without an end and without a beginning, just hanging, alone. His neck was awfully bruised, blue and purple with inflamed red tinges due to the strain of the rope.

We stopped and stared, horrified by the emptiness he had become.

'He's gone,' said Todd.

Chapter 23

I can never forget the day of Tony's funeral; it was so full of sadness and left a lasting impression on me. I could have sworn the entire community were present. There were so many people there weren't enough seats, people had to stand in the back row for the entire service. I don't think Tony understood how much of an impact he had on the community. Everyone loved him. They may not have shown it in a recognizable way, but they did.

There were old folks seated in the front rows, resting their elbows on their canes, who too, looked just about ready to fly away and leave this place behind—gracefully, I hoped. I could see within their ancient eyes they wished God took them instead of Tony. There was still so much life left for him to live. His journey had really only just begun. But he made the conscious decision to cut it short and end the ride.

I'll never forget when Tony's father stepped to the podium before the hundreds of watery eyed people. He looked like he hadn't slept in days since receiving the news. 'Firstly,' he said, 'I am blown away by the amount of people who showed up to celebrate the life of Tony. It goes to show how many people he had touched... I just wish that he could have seen this, maybe then, he wouldn't have done what he did...' He cleared his throat and scratched his eyes, trying to hold himself together. 'Since Tony was little, he was always such a loving and caring boy, these things were second nature to him. He had a mouthful of cheek and was at times difficult to deal with, but we loved him for it. He never had any trouble making friends—as you can see.' He gestured to the crowd. 'In the twenty years of his life he's achieved a lot—in fact, nearly twenty-one—Tony excelled in the Air Force cadets, he discovered school wasn't for him, much to his teachers dismay.' The auditorium echoed with laughter. 'He has always been an adventurous spirit, so adventurous one day he thought it was a good idea to take his Gran's car for a spin and pick up one of his buddies before crashing.' More laughter filled the auditorium. 'He has always been good with his hands, so he became a roofer, which allowed him to get his own place and learn independence. Later he decided roofing wasn't for him and he moved on...' His father closed his eyes and breathed heavily. 'And when his time would come, I knew he would have made an excellent husband and father... We love you so much and it really hurts us to see you go... I'm just sorry there wasn't anything we could do, and that we weren't there to show you there was another way...'

At the end of the funeral, we were able to see Tony for the last time in the funeral home. His white coffin was completely covered in loving messages written in permanent marker, there were so many scribbles I struggled to find a free space to write my own farewell.

He was dressed in a suit with a tie and his collars were pulled up higher than someone would usually wear a dress-shirt to cover the scars on his throat. But part of him was missing. As I stared at him and held his cold hand, I couldn't find him. He was no longer the funny, boisterous guy I knew and loved, but an empty vessel no longer occupied.

It was really hard for me to see my buddy like this, so I went outside to smoke a cigarette. When I went back in, I was surprised to see Jasmine and Tasha hovering over his coffin. They smiled weakly as they caught onto my presence, I stood at a respectful distance and let them bid him farewell. Tasha leaned in close and whispered, 'Goodbye my friend. I didn't know you too well. But you made me feel beautiful that night.' She then kissed him on the forehead, and they turned to leave.

At the end of the service, I donated a lump of money to his parents and saved one hundred dollars for two ferry tickets for me and Charlie. We spread his ashes in a lonesome river north of Upper Hutt, hoping it would carry him somewhere peaceful. Nothing was said as we watched his remains drift downstream, we were hollow like the shell he left behind.

It hit me later through the hours of manic mental pacing, where all I did was think... think of you...

clambering about the intricacies of each event of your life, searching for a plausible cause. Yet nothing. There was nothing to be found other than the pain you left me behind. But you found your peace. It took me a while, but I, too, found my own.

I carried around the pamphlet from the funeral that had his picture on it wherever I went, just like the way he used to carry around the picture of his mother. I soon learned why he did this. In some way he felt closer to me, like he was still walking alongside me. I decided I would carry his picture until I reached the South Island and leave it on the sands of Golden Bay, in essence, his spirit could experience the freedom we longed for.

I visited the same river where we spread Tony's ashes every day and sat on a pile of rocks watching the river rapids, knowing Tony was now a part of that ever flowing current. I listened to the water gargle as it struck the rocks, swearing I heard wisps of Tony's voice reassuring me he was okay.

When the sun began to wither behind the hills, I asked the same old question, *why*? Why did you have to go out in this way? Wasn't our friendship strong enough to withstand the storm which tore your foundation to the ground? Or did I fail you as a friend? I'll never know. Tony took these things with him and to his grave.

I didn't know much at the time; it was hard to see clearly when all I saw was the murky visions of the hundreds of thousands of others who shared the same struggles as he did. But what I did know was the sun would rise again, and I would use its light to navigate through the fog until I found my place, my home.

Some may call my plans to vacate south a means of escape but that was far from the truth. The world we were tangled up in wished to shove its disenchanted morals down our throats until we spoke with the same vehemence as them, and acted unjust, like them.

It is easier to bow to someone else's will as it is to oppose them. There was no ultimate goal the maddened world bestowed upon us other than self-indulgence, turning us into another crippled product floating down the conveyor belt of existence. It was hard to stand up and take ownership of my life and stare at myself in the mirror and say, *I was wrong*, but without taking responsibility for what my life had become how do I expect to change it? The path before me was terrifying, but without fear there is no courage, without courage there is only blind acceptance.

Chapter 24

I decided to leave at sunrise the following morning, however I couldn't show my face in town, the police were crawling all over the Hutt Valley looking to question me over the death of Ruby. Knowing the Dooley's, they'd pin some twisted story on me which would put me behind bars. Though, I'm sure the Dooley's would be hoping to get their hands on me first. I couldn't imagine how Connor felt. No doubt him and his mates wanted to deal with me first, then leave my battered remains in a sack outside the police station.

I felt lost with nowhere to go. The feelings reminded me of when Mr. Stevenson hunted me and Tony down in Totra Park after the incident with Joanna, and we had no other choice but to head for the hills.

That's what I'll do, I thought.

I remembered when we first arrived at the cabin Tony pointed out the Manaaki Falls trail on the adjacent hill. He said it went all the way to Eastbourne. From

Upper Hutt it would take us three days, four if Charlie didn't have appropriate footwear. Also, with the chilling nights we couldn't sleep in the open with only a sleeping bag, I needed a tent for further protection against the elements.

My backpack sprang to mind. Within it I had everything I ever needed to travel safely. I had a tent, guy ropes and a tarp, a warmer sleeping bag (Charlie could use it and I could use the lighter one Jacklyn let me borrow), tins of food in which that guy in Shakespeare Avenue gave me, that is if Clinton and his hoodlums hadn't eaten it all—not to mention if he hadn't already sold everything to Cash Converters.

Clinton routinely dropped into Jacklyn's place every night at 9PM to pick up weed for delivery runs. He practically lived out of the back of his wagon so surely the backpack hadn't travelled far. Normally, thugs like Blaze and Anthony were always waiting in the car as he went in to pick up the goods, so I had to tread carefully.

Before anything went down, I had to explain the plan to Charlie and Todd. Charlie was lying on Tony's mattress wearing his denim jacket, pondering the ceiling. I told her my plans and she was keen on every aspect, asides from hiking all the way there. In spite of how she felt, she scanned her phone for information about Manaaki Falls, and quickly found what we were looking for.

The trail started in Otaki and rambled over the rigid bushy shoulders of the Hutt Valley, ending in Eastbourne where a waterfall met the ocean. But if we climbed

Jacobs Ladder—a peak in Upper Hutt—we could merge with the halfway point on the Manaaki trail. We discovered there was a little ferry that regularly travelled between Eastbourne and the Wellington harbor. The plan was flawless, but only if I retrieved my backpack from Clinton.

'Start packing your things,' I said to Charlie. 'Essentials only, take what you can carry.'

She nodded and ran for the house.

'And Charlie,' I said. 'Be discreet, no one can know about our plans.'

Next, I went to find Todd. He was in his room playing PlayStation with Amos.

'We're leaving first thing tomorrow morning,' I told him.

'What? I thought you were taking the piss when you said you were running away.' He laughed awkwardly.

I nodded. 'I want you to come with us.'

'There's no way in hell I'm leaving my kid brother alone. He's not gonna go through what I had to endure growing up, not if I can help it.'

'Bring him with you—'

'The answer's no,' he said. 'Look, I disagree with a lot of things my mum does. But I can't take Amos away from her. He needs her. But eventually, as he grows up, he'll realize he doesn't.' He scrunched up his face. 'When did you say you were leaving?'

'Tomorrow morning.'

'I'd tread carefully around the Hutt Valley if I were you. Those rich douche-bags will have every cop in town on your tail.' He shook his head. 'And once mum finds out you bailed on her… let's just say it would suck to be you. You do plan on paying her back for the MDMA Tony gave away?'

'I don't have the money,' I replied. 'After donating to Tony's parents, all I have left is enough for two ferry tickets.'

'Shit, well you planned that right,' he said sarcastically. 'Mum wants to see you in the kitchen, anyway. You better have a believable excuse, because she's one unforgiving bitch when she wants to be… and for the record, this conversation never happened.'

As I walked toward the backyard, I heard wheels screeching and saw headlights dash over the trees. *Clinton*, I thought. I crouched behind an old oak tree as Chief went berserk behind the gate. Clinton and his goons jumped out and walked toward the back door. Wasting no time, I made my way in the direction of his car. Peering through the window I caught sight of a beat-up mattress in the boot along with what appeared to be a portable kitchen. *It's got to be in here*, I thought, opening the boot, rummaging through his stuff.

Eventually I found my backpack under one of the seats—or what was left of it. I tore the lid off various plastic containers withholding food, gas for the stove, and finally what he had stolen from me. So it seemed he never traded them into Cash Converters, but instead used them for camping. It didn't surprise me. Clinton was a bludger, a hustler who would go to extreme lengths to take people's money yet refused to pay his dues. In the same container was my sleeping bag, tent, guy ropes and tarp—also, I found a hunting knife and decided to bag it, thinking maybe it would come in handy during the days to come.

I hastily loaded the stuff into my pack keeping a close eye on the back door. The boys wouldn't be hanging around for too long. I crept through the back gate, actively announcing Chiefs name so he knew it was me. Chief still flew at me and furiously sniffed my shoes until he recognized my scent. From the other side of the backyard, I heard a twig snap and the old autumn leaves crunch in my direction. Then I heard a hushed murmur. 'Corey... over here, I need some help.' I heard wheels rolling over concrete, reminding me of brief visits to the airport when I was a kid. Charlie hauled an over-sized suitcase, dragging it along the grass and fallen oak leaves with all her strength. It turned out Charlie jumped out the bedroom window with all her stuff.

'You've got to be kidding...' I muttered.

Inside the garage, I lifted her suitcase to gain a general idea of its weight, not even an airport baggage service would accept her luggage without charging an additional fee.

'You do realize your gonna have to carry it up a hill,' I said.

'Yeah,' she replied, displaying not a doubt she could handle it.

I analysed her petite build and shrugged it off for the time being. 'So, you're an avid hiker?' I asked.

'I used to take a short cut through the hills to get to

school when I didn't have enough bus money. But that's about as far as my bush walking experience goes.'

'Right,' I said, whilst experiencing visions of myself dragging her Chariot-like suitcase uphill like a Roman soldier.

There was a bang on the door which rattled the entire garage. Charlie reacted at the speed of lightning and threw a blanket over her suitcase before the door flew open. It was Jacklyn. She was wearing a dressing gown with slippers and stepped into the garage with her arms crossed and a dank expression on her face.

'You know why I'm here,' she said angrily. 'You owe me some money!'

'I don't have it,' I said. 'I donated the last of my money to Tony's foster parents.'

'Bullshit!' she exclaimed. 'Don't lie to me, someone's going to have to pay it forward… Tony certainly can't, so it's gotta be you! You've got until tomorrow morning. Better hit the drawing board, guys.' She shot an awful look at Charlie, then smiled sinisterly. 'Maybe you can put Charlie to good use, whore her out on the streets. That seems to be all she's good for!'

'Fuck you and fuck this prison of a home, you selfish bitch!' Charlie screamed. 'Tony's dead and all you care about is getting your money back. What kind of person does that make you?'

Jacklyn stormed toward her and raised her hand, slapping her in the face with a thundering clap. 'How dare you speak to me like that! After everything I've done for you!' She turned her rage back on me. 'Keep this little whore of yours in line, Corey. I want my money by tomorrow, otherwise Todd and the boys will dig you a grave beside Tony's.'

'Fucking bitch!' Charlie shouted as we watched her leave. 'Who does she think she is—'

'We need to go, now!' I said. 'Make sure you've got everything, I'm getting Todd.'

I pounded on Todd's door one last time.

'What is it now?' he asked, all red eyed and drowsy.

'We're leaving right now and you're coming with us. I won't take no for an answer, Todd. You and I both know you're better off without this cancer in your life. I can see it eating away at you.'

'I told you,' he said, 'I'm not bailing on my kid brother. If I leave him, he'll go through exactly what I went through, and that's not happening...'

My voice softened. 'Just come with us,' I pleaded.

'Get out of here, Corey!' he demanded, unable to shake the tears forming in his eyes. 'I don't want to see your face around town ever again... If I do—the things I'll have to do to you... go! Get out of here!'

We stared into each other's eyes. Time seemed to stop as I suddenly realized this chapter of my life was finally about to close.

***

Avoiding the main roads, we cut through the railway yard in the dead of night and slipped under a broken fence leading to Maidstone park. After passing through a neglected cemetery full of turned over headstones, we scrambled up a grassy hill that quickly became speckled with pine trees and dense bush. In no time the sparkling lights of town seemed to get smaller as our footpath became a thin trail of dirt. There were no more streetlights to guide us, trail markers became our only source of guidance.

I was exhausted after lugging Charlie's suitcase up hill. The flashlight on her phone was draining her battery and we already took the wrong route two times before having to backtrack, so I decided to pitch the tent and call it a night. Due to being halfway up an incline there was no levelled ground to get a good pitch, so we ended up setting up the tent on a 45-degree angle.

Once we hunkered into our sleeping bags with too much on our minds to talk, I wondered if I had made the right decision for both of us. All I ever wanted in life was to find peace, I didn't know, let alone understand at the age of twenty we all had to travel down a rocky road in order to find the elusive sense of peace. We would be challenged. The past would try and hold us back, tempting us with the same old road we've walked down thousands of times before, knowing where every fork in the road would lead, knowing what dangers resided around the corner, and all the right places to hide to avoid being found by our fears.

Once it hit dawn, we began the tiresome climb to the summit. The vegetation grew scarce in the same way it did when we approached the cabin. From afar, the clusters of pine melded into a canvas of forest green, as if it were a portrait hanging on a wall. We dropped our packs at the Manaaki Falls signpost and collapsed to the dirt, using our shirts to wipe the sweat off our face. The gruelling climb was finally over, now, all we had to do was follow the galloping ridges to the harbor. From the top of Jacobs Ladder I could see the vague stillness of the ocean, it was close enough to admire its colour, but too far to perceive movement and landmarks.

'Beautiful, isn't it,' I said.

Charlie was facing the opposite direction, admiring the views of the town we left behind. She pulled out a bottle of water from her suitcase. 'Yeah, it is,' she said. 'From this view nobody would expect such horrible things to be going on down there.' She took a drink. 'Maybe this is what God sees and he's oblivious to our suffering.'

'If there is a God he definitely knows, I'll tell you that much,' I said.

We took turns chugging down the water until our cotton dry throats were satisfied and carried on through the wavering hills. I constantly had to change arms to compensate for the weight of the suitcase. My arms were cramping from heaving it up and down the ridge too many times to count. Lugging the bastard downhill was the worst, the wheels would always slip on the rocks and whack into the back of my ankles, making our progress strenuous and painfully minimal. The plastic wheels weren't designed for dirt and rocky rubble, in no time they snapped off and I had to drag the suitcase like it was a treasure chest.

'I can't do this for much longer,' I grumbled.

'Let's swap then,' she said.

She was already struggling carrying the backpack, there was no way she could drag her suitcase for another day and a half. She insisted on carrying her baggage with her, but after half an hour she couldn't go on any further.

'You're gonna have to lighten the load,' I said.

'How am I going to do that?' she asked.

'By throwing away some stuff.'

She stared at her suitcase thoughtfully. 'No. I need everything. My whole life is in that suitcase, throwing away something is like screwing up a part of my life and turfing it.'

'There will be things in your suitcase that no longer serve you, and things you need to let go,' I said. 'If you throw away what you no longer need it will make room for new things relevant to your life, things that will assist you rather than weigh you down.'

After much debate she decided to sift through her baggage and throw away her attachments to the past. She realized there were more than a few things she held onto. Charlie ended up discarding over half of her suitcase, leaving it in a pile at the side of the trail. With all her baggage behind her, she moved freely up the crest.

The hills were deserted yet full of life. From up here life appeared to be amplified. The furious gusts soared in from the coast and swept through the valley, forcing us to lean our body weight forward as we were nearly knocked off our feet in the exposed regions. The path meandered over the hills as far as the eye could see, seemingly moving further away from us through each step. If I focused my attention on the distant path, I found myself struggling to harness the strength to carry on. So I focused on putting one foot in front of the other, present with the dirt beneath my feet, feeling every strain in my calves, every dull ache in my spine, until I found my rhythm.

At the end of the day, we reached flat ground and stumbled across a partly burnt tree. Charlie gathered a handful of dried twigs and I laboriously ripped off meaty branches and used my foot to snap them into pieces. We stacked rocks in a circle around the twigs and used a book Charlie had brought to start the fire. Once we got it going, Charlie eagerly fed the fire with the branches, obsessively prodding at the embers with a stick to keep it a light. Our fire nearly went out twice, but Charlie attended to it, focusing all of her attention as if it were our last remaining flicker of hope to hold onto.

Entranced by the fire, we listened to the crackling twigs as the smoke wavered to the sky and enjoyed a smoke, watching the stillness of nature. I couldn't contain what I'd bottled inside of me any longer. If there was a time to let it all out, it was now. I had been holding onto every one of Tony's last words he said to me, reciting them to myself every second I had alone. Finally, I released it all. 'It should have been me,' I said, sobbing into my shirt sleeve. 'Tony said it himself, if we never met none of this would have happened—he'd still be alive! If I put my foot down at Connors party, and said we were going, none of this would have happened… I'm sick of life and all its consequences. I can't do anything without receiving a reaction, a reaction that changes everything... I just want to find a place where no one knows my name. I... I can't grow here. The past is always holding me back.'

'Who do you want to be, Corey?' asked Charlie.

"I don't know, anything but *them*.'

'Who?'

'Those people who waltz around town thinking they know everyone's business, but they don't know shit about me or Tony—or the reasons why we had to do what we had to do.'

Charlie wrapped her arm around me and pulled me into her breast. She said nothing, and nothing needed to be said, I just needed someone to understand, someone to be there for me.

Cradling me in her arms she began to hum a melody, then she sung sweetly.

Everyone needs some Manaaki... when you're feeling sad...
Everyone needs a friend... When you're feeling bad...
Everyone needs some Manaaki...'

She sung until my tears stopped pouring and turned to a gradual drip.

'My mother used to sing that to me when I was little... before she got sick. Don't worry about what everyone else thinks. If you hold onto what others think of you, eventually you'll become the person they see. As long as we make our reaction a positive one, everyone's life will change for good...'

She was right. I failed to understand the meaning of

these natural laws at this time of my life. My youthful soul was too angry at the world, too hurt, to know any different. It wasn't until later in life I learned what Charlie was trying to say. In life we cannot be defined by what happens to us, but rather by how we react to what happens to us.

'I couldn't have made it this far without you,' I said.

'I don't know where I would be if I didn't meet you and Tony,' she said, averting her eyes to the stars. 'For the first time in my life, I feel hope, like I can actually be someone other than the girl everyone expected me to become. We're nearly there. The freedom of a new land awaits us, and it's not going anywhere any time soon.'

We had to bleed from our feet before we could reach our destination. Nothing worth fighting for came easy. There was always an internal war, a battle in which we can't always expect to win. But through losing we are granted the skills to achieve our goals. The provided insights would never have come to us if all we ever did was win. Even when I would lose, I knew there was something to be gained. It may not have been a medal to remind me of my successes, but a silent call to try again.

Chapter 25

Perched on the edge of a rocky ridge we nestled into our sleeping bags, fully dressed, trying to find comfort on the bumpy nylon floor. The frames of the tent rattled terrifyingly in the wind, the mighty pines swayed and danced as the wind whistled through the leaves, wooing like a spirit residually haunting the land. Outside those four nylon walls was a wild world modern man was incapable of conquering—like the wayward unconscious, the all-encompassing gloom—and each of us were the tiny lantern held by the wise old man.

'I'm scared,' Charlie whispered, pulling her sleeping-bag up to her chin.

The tent shook so aggressively I was convinced someone was outside shaking it. I popped my head out the flap and was greeted by the void. We were cradled on the edges of Manaaki's shoulder, waiting for him to raise his hands of clay and brush us off, as if we were insignificant like a fly.

Blocking out the formidable forces of nature, I lay my head on my backpack, praying sleep would take me to safety. The howling wind loosened its hold on me as I fell through the layers of myself, landing in the weightlessness of my dreams.

I rubbed my eyes, surprised to feel the warmth of a fireplace against my skin. I unzipped my sleeping bag and stepped to the creaky wooden floorboards. On either side of me were empty bunkbeds, and to my surprise, I saw Tony's denim jacket left to dry by the fireplace. Tony burst through the door; his hands full of kindling he gathered from the back of the cabin.

It can't be, I thought.

He grinned as if intercepting my thoughts. He dropped the pile of wood to the floor. 'It's about time you woke up,' he said.

Astounded, I said, 'Tony... what are you doing here?'

I noticed he was dressed in the same black jacket, shirt and tie he was wearing at his funeral, but he no longer bared the scars around his neck.

'I could ask you the same thing,' he replied. 'I've got to tell you something, and you better listen—by the way, the two of you have done a good job so far, but remember, you are not there yet.'

I shook my head in disbelief. He seemed so animated and lively, just like I remembered.

'Dude... how did you get here?'

'Don't think too much of it,' he said. 'Otherwise, you'll wake yourself up. As I was saying, once you arrive in the city, head straight to the ferry terminal, buy your tickets and stay there. Promise me you won't go wandering off.'

'I promise,' I said.

'Good. Now go back to your bunk and get some sleep, you'll need it.'

The moment I processed what he said I felt a surge of electricity light up the base of my spine. It climbed up my back and lingered around my head. Immense pressure weighed heavy on my mind. I screamed, convinced my head was going to explode.

'Corey, it's okay,' said Charlie. 'You're just having a bad dream.'

I propelled out of my sleeping bag, sweating profusely.

'We have to go,' she said. 'It's a beautiful day for walking, spring is on its way!'

I thought about the dream of Tony, but as I aligned myself with the waking world it quickly faded into the back of my mind. Without giving it any second thoughts, I helped Charlie pack up our things before setting foot on the declining path to Manaaki Falls.

Charlie wasn't wrong about the weather, the sky was blue and cloudless, birds fluttered around us welcoming spring with their songs. The fog had dissipated, no longer polluting our vision with uncertainty.

The coast was within our sights. Below us, to the right, was the town of Lower Hutt tucked comfortably into the valley, and to our left was Wainuiomata blanketed with lush green ferns. We stopped and stared in awe as we made out the buildings in Wellington city, reaching up to the overseeing hills like urban pinnacles.

Late into the afternoon, we arrived at Manaaki Falls when the sun was beginning to collapse into the ocean. The waterfall wasn't as profound as I envisioned and could easily pass off as a rapid flowing creek, but it didn't dampen our accomplishment, nor did it hinder its beauty. We had made it and that was all that mattered.

I stood in front of the lake running in-between the foot of two hills. A thin river ran through the peaks which eventually led to the ocean. I had my fair share of burdens, like many youthful souls who were full of questions and on a quest for greater meaning. In this moment, I discovered nature more than often soothed my troublesome mind, whether it was the way the fresh air purified my polluted lungs, or the space it offered, happy to be silent when I wanted solitude, but also happy to interact when I wanted company. In the past, the city put a strain on my wondering mind, and quite often turned me into a machine devoid of the very thing I was searching for; purpose.

As Charlie rested on the lakeside watching the butterflies flutter around her, I picked up a stone and threw it into the lake, watching it disappear into the elusive waters. Despite the stone vanishing, never to be seen again, the impact shook the water and created small waves that rippled out among the entire lake. The ripples crept down the river between the hills, and finally met the ocean. It was then, for the first time, I heard the language of nature. Unlike a teacher who enforced their authority of knowledge upon a student, nature remained silent, enabling a moments contemplation so one could dig deep into themselves to unearth their version of truth. After a moment of meditation, I could fathom the vision nature painted. The vision did not offer a solution to my problems, but an insight, an insight that was strong enough to give me the courage to return to the city, and the strength to start again.

Chapter 26

Early the next morning we waited at the edge of a brittle wharf for the ferry. There was nothing to suggest the frequency of the service other than a slanting, graffiti signpost stating the price of the fares, which looked like teenagers had took to it with a bat. In the distance I could see Somes Island, the first stop on the ferry before Queens Wharf. We were the only commuters, which made me wonder if the service was still in operation.

However, a little ferry pulled into the wharf half an hour later and we found a seat at the top of the deck.

'Tickets please,' said the old ticket master.

I was too caught up in our next move I had forgotten completely about money. All I had was enough for the Inter-Islander. I shrugged and looked over to Charlie.

'How much?' Charlie asked, fumbling around in her suitcase.

'Six-fifty each,' he replied.

After pulling her bag apart and rummaging through

all the compartments, Charlie managed to find a five dollar note. She handed it to the ticket master with her head down.

'I'm sorry, but it's all we've got.'

The old ticket master screwed up his face and glanced over his shoulder. We were the only ones on the top deck, in fact, the only ones on the ferry. He looked us over. We were dressed in the same clothes from the day we left Upper Hutt, our faces glazed over with sweat, shining like grease in the sun, dirt and dust speckled over our jackets, our hair and shoes. He glanced at Charlie's beat-up suitcase that looked like it had been through a war zone.

'Where you heading?' he asked.

'To the city,' Charlie replied.

The old ticket master sighed and shook his head. 'This is only going to happen once.' He took her money and handed us two tickets.

Not long after, the ferry docked on Queens Wharf and we shuffled along the pier toward the Inter-Islander terminal to buy our tickets. Unfortunately, we were a minute too late and missed the morning service to Picton. The next service was expected to depart at 1PM.

We lounged around the deserted terminal having more time to kill than two people could handle. For the next hour we gazed at the arrival and departure screen obsessively, as if expecting our ferry to arrive any minute.

'I'm going to clean myself up,' said Charlie. 'I've got to get out of these clothes. I suggest you do the same, we don't want to draw any attention to ourselves.'

'I don't have any other clothes,' I said. 'All I've got is the clothes on my back.'

'Typical guy,' she said, dusting off the dirt trapped within the creases of my leather jacket. 'At least brush your teeth,' she added, as she strolled down the corridor to the bathroom.

In the bathroom, I splashed water over my face, and ran my fingers through my disobedient blond hair. I caught my eyes in the mirror and stared for what felt like an eternity. I barely recognized myself. I was a world away from the person I was before stepping out of the city, so hopeless, steeped in poverty and ongoing tragedy. I felt out of touch with my former self, like the way someone loses contact with an old friend. I couldn't identify who was staring back at me. Who was he? A sleaze? A scumbag? A cheat? Or was he a good Samaritan? A leader? Or the good Christian boy his foster mother always wanted him to be. In fact, I had been all of them at least once in my life.

I saw a flash of familiarity within those blue eyes. He looked like the wiser version of myself after all the lessons of youth had been taught, learned, and repeated. The person staring back at me was capable of taking ownership of their life, he could have played the victim, he could have wallowed in self-induced depression, but instead, he chose to take responsibility for his life, to be held accountable for everything he had done, good or bad. He was a man. An adult. A survivor against all odds, free to be whatever he wanted to be. He was me.

As I killed time, I had a crazy idea to hit the streets to

find Homeless Harry. I knew all his favourite hang-out spots—not to mention I knew the city like the palm of my hand. There were too many people to make me noticeable, too many cultures, trends, and fashions to keep track of. Charlie returned from the bathroom looking like a different girl, her long black hair went all bushy and curly from the exposure to the elements in the hills, now, it was silky and straight, her make-up done like she was about to hit the town.

'What a transformation,' I said, smirking. 'I think I liked your hair better before, wild and free.'

'Wish I could say the same about you,' she replied, smiling.

'You look good when you smile,' I said. 'You should do it more often.'

She blushed and said, 'No one's said that to me before.'

'Well, maybe you just haven't surrounded yourself with the kind of people who notice these things.'

'Yeah, maybe…' Charlie said, reflectively gazing at her shoes.

Changing the subject, I said, 'I'm heading out to the city, gonna find Homeless Harry to say goodbye one last time.'

'Okay, I'm coming too.'

'No, you're not!'

'Ah, yeah, I am. You can't tell me what to do!'

'It's for the best,' I said. 'Trust me.'

'I knew Homeless Harry just as much as he knows you,' she said angrily.

'You've got to trust me, Charlie.'

'I do,' she replied. 'I wouldn't have followed you through the hills if I didn't.'

I put my hand on her shoulder. 'Then believe me when I say you're safer here.'

She looked like she was about to explode with more reasons why she should come with me, but nonetheless she sat down, putting her feet up on the unoccupied seats, and pretended she didn't know me.

'You've got two hours,' she said as I was leaving. 'Please don't do anything stupid.'

'I'll be back—I promise!'

***

I followed the boardwalk around the pier, quickly becoming another faceless voyager caught in the city rip. At this hour, there was no time to stop and admire the salty ocean air, everyone was too busy checking their watches, slamming back coffee like it was shots of tequila, late for their morning meetings as they marched in formation to their corporate caves.

For a moment, I sat to the side of the foot traffic and stared out at the bay. I had seen this view too many times for it to be special, more so, it reminded me of a dark time in my life now behind me. To put it quite plainly, nothing had changed in the city, nothing would, it was, and still is, a psychic dumping ground.

I couldn't wait to hear Homeless Harry's deep, calm collected voice say, *"As long as your heart's in the right place—and you've got plenty of it, you'll be fine, kid. Just don't go giving your heart away to the takers of the world, they'll rob you blind. Save your heart for the people who need it the most. There's a lot of hurting people out there, but I believe your heart is big enough to heal everyone of 'em… Stay strong, kid. Don't let the beat bring you down, remember, life is just one great big song…"*

I walked deeper into the city treading in the shadows of skyscrapers, everywhere I looked I saw clocks, a reminder time is money, money is time, and time was hungry. Once I escaped the corporate offices along Featherston Street I linked onto Cuba, where frail hostels were pushed downtown, an inviting place for backpackers looking for a cheap bed.

Outside the hostel there were scruffy nomads wearing woollen jumpers resting their backs on bricks, solemnly smoking the day away as they watched the commuters run a marathon around the clock. Next to the hostel was the downtown homeless shelter where Harry spent most of his time when he wasn't on the streets busking.

As I approached the entrance, the strange dream I had the night before bombarded my mind. Tony's warning to not go further than the ferry terminal played on repeat, but I brushed it off as some deep seeded fear being projected into my dreams.

The clerk to the homeless shelter greeted me at reception, offering me tea and biscuits. 'I'm sorry,' the clerk said, 'we are full at the moment—always are during winter, but come back in a few days, the shelter tends to thin out throughout the coming of spring.'

'I'm not after a bed,' I said.

He ignored me. 'Actually,' the clerk interrupted, shuffling through various papers on his desk. 'There's one bed available, must be your lucky day.'

I checked the clock on the wall. The ferry was expected to depart in an hour, so I cut right to the chase. 'I'm here to see Harry, often referred to as Homeless Harry.'

The clerk looked a little sick and awkwardly rose to his feet. 'Are you family?'

'Yeah, I guess you could say that.'

He took a deep breath and gestured for me to take a seat beside the water cooler. 'Uh, I don't know how to say this, but Harry unfortunately passed away a couple of nights ago. He died of natural causes—and from what the doctors told me, he passed peacefully. I'm terribly sorry.'

I didn't know whether to laugh or cry, so I did both.

'You're the first family member to visit him in a long time,' he said. 'Follow me, I left everything the way it was in his locker, please, take whatever you like.' I followed him down a rickety corridor with rusted lockers on either side of the walls. He handed me a set of keys. 'I'll be at reception if you need me, take as long as you like.'

I thanked him and rummaged through Harry's locker. I found a large tobacco tin; it was heavy and rattled and clinked. I opened it, my jaw dropping at the sight of gold coins and bundles of notes Harry had collected from his jam sessions. I tucked the tin into my jacket pocket. Then I went straight for a large hard case and unclipped the hinges. Inside was Harry's pride and joy, his sacred sax. It seemed to light up the darkened hall, it was carefully polished and nurtured like a divine relic. Within the interior of the soft, felt-brushed casing was a fraying sheet of paper. It was the notations to the song he wrote called *Wellington City Blues*.

I remembered sitting on the curb when he first wrote the song as I translated his grooves into words, calling the poem: *City Blues*. Homeless Harry loved every word of it, telling me if his song had a voice this is exactly what it would be saying. I teared up as the reality of his death chiselled through my heart. I tucked the notations back into the case and carefully placed it back into his locker.

'Rest in peace my friend,' I whispered. 'Thank you— for everything.'

Chapter 27

Without a minute to spare I made my way back to the pier. I was already running late, Charlie would be wondering where the hell I was, but at this pace I'd manage to get to the terminal just as people started boarding.

I sprinted along the boardwalk, so close to the docks I could hear the distant clang of a ships bell. It was then I saw him. But he saw me first. Sitting outside Macs Brewery on the wooden benches were three people I hoped to never see again. Immediately, I recognized his blond wavy fringe combed back, and the far away glimmer in his cold blue eyes, foretelling he had seen death, and death still loomed over him, not mournfully however, but it hung over him with a vengeance.

Connor's hateful eyes stuck to me as he leaped off the bar stall and blocked the path, narrowing my escape. He was just as surprised to see me as I was to see him. Liam and Shag stood staunchly at his side, creating an impenetrable formation.

I could have spun around and ran in the opposite direction, but I was done with running away from my problems. Feeling my heart gnaw through my chest, I slowly approached them. Connor leered at me like an animal eying its prey, his bottom lip trembling with sadness, his eyes lusting to see my insides sprawled out on the pavement.

'Connor,' I began, 'I'm sorry about what happened to Ruby. It wasn't our fault. It could have happened to anyone.'

'Wasn't your fault?!' he blurted. 'None of this would have happened if you didn't come to my house that night!'

I took a step back, holding my hands up. 'I know there's nothing I can say or do to make this situation any better. But I'm sorry. Two people died because of what happened that night.'

'Tony deserved to die!' Connor said scornfully. 'But Ruby… that's bullshit!'

My heart sunk. 'No, he didn't. Do you know why he took his life? Because he couldn't cope with the fact, he took someone else's. Tony didn't deserve to die; Ruby didn't deserve to die… this is just a fucked-up situation that got out of hand.'

'A fucked-up situation that got out of hand,' Connor repeated nodding his head incessantly. 'Fuck you! The two of you are murderers! Tony's lucky he's dead, because I would have killed him, too… but that's okay, you'll get double treatment to make up for it!'

'You don't wanna do this,' I said. 'It's not going to make anything better.'

Ignoring me, the boys advanced. Shag put me into a headlock and steered me down an alley and into the loading zone of the brewery. He threw me like a ragdoll into a heap of empty kegs which scattered like bowling pins.

'Get the fuck up!' Connor shouted. He was no longer himself, but a demon who yearned for broken bones and swollen purple skin.

Despite my best efforts I couldn't move, my body refused to stop shaking. Shag grabbed me by the collars on my jacket and pulled me to my feet. Connor stepped forward and began to throw vicious jabs into my gut, knocking the wind out of me as I bent over my knees. Shag then took me from behind and held me upright like I was a boxing bag. Next, it was Liam's turn. He threw a rabid right across my face, sending me airborne and into a puddle. He coughed up phlegm and spat in my face before proceeding to boot my ribs senselessly.

Connor hovered above me. 'Don't you look at me like that, Corey,' he said. 'You deserve this!'

My legs were so battered I couldn't gather the strength to stand on my own two feet. Shag took great amusement in this and unzipped the fly to his jeans and pissed on me. 'This is exactly what I think of you,' he said, laughing. 'But you're not even worth the piss trickling out my cock!'

'Get him up!' Connor demanded.

Liam and Shag followed his orders, each of them

grabbing one of my arms and steadying me to my feet.

'How does it feel?' asked Connor.

I spat blood at him. 'How does what feel?'

'To kill someone. I bet you get a rush... sorta like MDMA, the MDMA you sold Ruby.'

'But it was you...' I said. 'You made her take the pill. She looked nervous, but you made her take it.'

'Liar!' Connor shouted. 'Don't spin this around—'

'Don't play the victim, when you and I both know who the victim really was.'

'Are you all there?' asked Connor, knocking on his head. 'You should have wrapped a rope around your neck and jumped ship with Tony... at least now he's at peace with his whore mother—'

Using the last of my strength I threw myself at Connor, busting his nose with my fist. There was blood everywhere. It poured out of his nose like a tap. He stopped and stared at the blood on his hands, shocked by my impulsive, swift attack. By the looks of it, I may have broken his nose, his perfect nose. Like most Dooley's, Connor was full of pride, too much he wouldn't go down without me going down first. His face turned into fire, he appeared to double in size, possessed by a primal rage I had only seen in people when they reached their breaking point. This even scared Shag and Liam, who cowered away in the corner.

Connor jabbed me in the head. I blocked it, but I couldn't stop the second blow coming from his other hand. One punch was all it took—I was already dazed from having my head and ribs stomped on. The fight was over. But not for Connor. He bounced around my immobile body and booted me until all I felt was pain pulsate through my body, his pain he projected upon me.

'Connor,' Shag said in a timid voice he rarely used. 'I think he's got the message.'

Connor refused, and proceeded to stomp on me like he was trying to put out a fire.

Shag persisted. 'You've taken this too far—you're really hurting him!'

'Do I look like I give a shit!' shouted Connor. He was wide eyed, maddened, as blood dripped from his crooked nose.

'He's right,' Liam broke in, 'this has gone too far…'

Unable to de-escalate Connor, and out of fear of their reputation being sullied by a criminal record, Shag and Liam legged it into the city. I closed my eyes, seeing nothing but my world fold over itself, convinced I had finally met my end, and now, I was ready for my beginning… Yet nothing but empty thoughts filled my mind, bleak visions of blackened skies filling up the fishbowl we called existence. My fishbowl was shaking, spilling over the edges as I trickled down into the infinite. But suddenly found by cold water being poured over my face.

I opened my eyes and wondered why a truck was reversing in my direction. Why did my torso feel like it had been through a meat grinder? The truck backing toward me halted. A man dressed in high visibility overalls was pouring a bottle of water over my face. 'Hey buddy,' he said. 'You've been in some kind of accident, but you're safe now. Help is on its way.'

'Accident?' I asked as recollections whirled inside of my head. 'This was no accident!'

'Calm down,' he said. 'Someone will be here to help real quick.'

To me help only meant one thing; cops and questions.

'What's the time?' I asked.

Startled, the man said, 'Half past three.'

Shit, I've been out for a couple of hours, I thought. Charlie—the ferry, I've missed it!

Ignoring the dispatch workers helpful gestures, I picked myself off the ground and staggered down the boardwalk to the terminal. Charlie was nowhere in sight. She left no sign, no clue, no trace. She had taken my backpack with her expecting me to board during the final seconds before departure. I swore and went to the bathrooms to clean myself up.

Thankful to still have the money I retrieved from Homeless Harry's locker, I limped to the ticket booth and dropped two handfuls of gold coins along with a couple of stray notes on the counter without bothering to count it. The lady in the ticket booth dropped her jaw when she saw me but didn't bother to ask any questions. 'One ticket on the next ferry,' I demanded.

She took her time counting all the coins and chump change. 'I just need a few details for your boarding pass, your full name for starters.'

'Corey Gnosis,' I said.

She rapidly typed it up, halted, and stared

thoughtfully into space. 'A young lady left this note for you before she boarded the 1PM service.' She slid it across the table. 'Here's your boarding pass, please take a seat over there, the ferry departs in two hours.'

I unfolded the slip of paper.

Dear Corey,
I don't know where you are, or what happened to you. But I hope you're safe. As you probably already know, I've taken your backpack just in case you board in the last second. If you are reading this, you've obviously missed the ferry. I do hope you get over here, hopefully they can refund your ticket. You will find me in Motueka.
Love Charlie

I smiled to myself, happy to know she had made it. Now it was my time. The journey was arduous with many setbacks, but I had made it. It didn't go as planned but life never does, the envisioned path always has, and will forever stray away into the pathways unknown to man.

The ferry was set to dock in two hours, in the meantime I lay down on a row of seats relaxing my decrepit body. Though, I wasn't as bad as I thought. The amount of blood that soaked into my t-shirt made my wounds look fatal, but asides from a few cracked ribs and a black eye I was alright. As I lay down, I thought about Charlie, she'd be well past the Cook Strait by now.

I found myself captivated by the departure/arrival screen once again, which did nothing for me other than cause a great deal of impatience. I decided to snooze for an hour or so, eventually being woken up by an automated voice announcing that the ferry had arrived. On deck, I found a quiet seat in a corner, dimmed the lights and slept for most of the journey.

The tipsy waves knocked the ferry around like a violent drunk brawling outside a pub, but somehow, I managed to get some sleep.

I woke up as the ferry cruised along the waters unhurriedly. The ferry drew closer inland, spectacular views of cliffs backing onto wondrous, rigid mountains came into sight. Behind me the sun was setting, burning out like the lantern I left behind in Wellington, the guiding light I had outgrown and could no longer follow.

Back home, I thought I could stand tall alongside the faces of the past, but as I came to realize, my knees were trembling in the void of the present. The absence of the present was like being without company, and this only meant there was nothing for me to create, no future for me in that old town.

Once the ferry docked in Picton, I followed a pedestrian path to the town centre. The place was practically deserted, it was one of those towns where everyone arrived only to leave, and I too would leave, but not before climbing the hill that overlooked the channel I had travelled to get here.

I sat on the grass at the top of the hill and stared out at the sky bursting with orange and yellow. There were darkening blue hues about to consume the remains of the sun. It was a hopeful horizon that somehow reminded me of Tony and Homeless Harry, fading out with the last light of the day.

I watched the ferry backtrack through the northern channel until all I saw was a little ball of light. I felt the end was near. In retrospect, my journey south was like a loosely tied knot that wasn't perfect, but it somehow held my life together. I reflected on my life back in Wellington, wanting to experience it all so it could be understood, folded and closed.

I watched the trees shake in the coastal breeze, wildflowers swayed rhythmically in open fields, lulled by the coming of spring, the wholesome moon hung low and proud in the diminishing sky. I turned my back on the northern horizons and retraced my steps down hill. As I stepped onto the open road, one thing occurred to me; if there is a beginning, then first there must be an end, for the end marks the beginning…

City Blues

Vultures dressed in suits peer down from the urban canopy, eying up their next meal. Meanwhile, awakening city dreamers and square eyed conservatives march downtown with laptop bags strapped over one shoulder, peering glumly into the horizon of grey bleakness, trapped in the confinements of Wednesday, waiting for the good news of Friday, with nothing to feel, lost in yesterday's dream because they forgot how to, so they learned to lean onto someone else's.

Hopeful hobos rise from beneath grimy blankets propelling off their concrete mattress, getting to work early, setting up their cardboard signs outside of banks, visualizing gold coins dropping. But the commuters are caught in the current, lost in the static of billboard vibrations. They're running late, flapping about in the city rip, drifting into the mouth of their weekly cage with a conscience full of mortgage debt, credit cards, and income, plastic dreams overlapping wondrous escapades.

Day suddenly falls into night like a curtain dropping over a brightly lit stage. The night wraps its claws around the dwellers beneath the moon, the same moon who governs the uncanny force of emotions.

As if blacking out and warping into unfamiliar territory, I find myself watching keen eyed lads who bob their heads in the back end of clubs, eying up the evening's potential. On the streets, moonlight hustlers sway with the coastal breeze, hands in pockets, eager to get the blood off their hands.

Dope pushers push up bras! Eighteen and free strutting down the main drag. A suburban nobody, a self-acclaimed big city alley cat, on the prowl lustfully licking their lips. Just another university girl with nothing to lose other than a few brain cells she didn't really need anyway. No bra, no sense—who needs sense nowadays—no windy Wellington gust caressing her nearly naked flesh, oblivious to her pink nippled twins who popped out wishing to see the city for themselves.

Opposite the clubs are an array of sleazy strip clubs with convulsive neon lights: 'Girls Girls Girls', and there's a lot of those dreamy girls replicated from small handheld screens, bending over on alcohol-stained tables like they dropped a hundred bucks in coins.

Back on Main Street, midnight missionaries who washed up from some American shore, watch on in horror seeing no more than the devil alive and breathing in the heart of midnight Wellingtonians.

Hymns refused or discarded, scrunched up and tossed to the sidewalk, collected by bums who spark flame to paper, warming up their bones to beat the city blues.

At the head of some lousy bar, tension is brewing. Half a dozen vodkas later, sanity hangs loosely around young men's necks, there's a push, a scuffle, sanity necklace breaks loose trampled on by weary feet.

Monkey out of cage, red eyes flaring with rage, now beaten to a limp carcass. Bystanders shrug it off, after all its just another soulless meat suit left to eat glass on the pavement. In the distance sirens are wailing, people fleeing, women screaming, paddy wagons sagging, Wellington city blues sombre and true, blowing notes that'll cause pineal glands to spasm, old folks to lock their doors and pull their blinds, teenagers to shrug and sink into the realms of their phones.

The cosmic curtain which once fell over this mistaken land begins to slowly lift. The lazy sun eventually rises over the harbor, accompanied by last night's regrets and misfortunes. The animals of night seek refuge in dimly lit bedrooms, hidden away from the day's illuminations, todays realizations, they can wait until tomorrow...

But life will go on, time moves too fast to stop. Those who move too slowly will perish in the city rip.

Homeless Harry looks down from above, enthralled by the immensity of life, all the people living and dying simultaneously collapsing into earth. It's all just one vast cosmic sea of vibrations, rippling out into universes upon universes yet to be seen through 21st century eyes. Yet all that is seen is tens of thousands of city eyes, finding their solace underneath nocturnal skies.

The train rolls on and out of town, traveling to a place where a different kind of song sweeps over the bushy hills, and down the valley like a tainted waterfall flooding the land, drowning out the sounds of the children's cries.

"Written by Corey Gnosis, while listening to Homeless Harry's Wellington City Blues"

Lightning Source UK Ltd.
Milton Keynes UK
UKHW040720150622
404461UK00001B/20